JANE LOVEI

THE BOYS OF CHRISTMAS

Complete and Unabridged

LINFORD
Leicester

First published in Great Britain in 2016 by
Choc Lit Limited
Surrey

First Linford Edition
published 2018
by arrangement with
Choc Lit Limited
Surrey

A catalogue record for this book is available
from the British Library.

ISBN 978–1–4448–3686–8

Published by
F. A. Thorpe (Publishing)
Anstey, Leicestershire

Set by Words & Graphics Ltd.
Anstey, Leicestershire
Printed and bound in Great Britain by
T. J. International Ltd., Padstow, Cornwall

This book is printed on acid-free paper

THE BOYS OF CHRISTMAS

When Mattie Arden receives a letter a few days before Christmas informing her that she has inherited a house from her great-aunt Millie, it's a welcome distraction. Except it comes with a strange proviso: if Mattie wants the house, she must fulfil Millie's last wish and scatter her ashes over 'the boys of Christmas'. In the company of her best friend Toby, Mattie sets out for the seaside village of Christmas Steepleton in the hope of finding out the meaning of her aunt's bizarre request . . .

I love Christmas.
So this book is dedicated to my
family, without whom Christmas
just wouldn't be the same — and
Brussels sprouts, because ditto.

Acknowledgements

This isn't a real acknowledgment as such. I'm just letting you know that fifteen per cent of the earnings from this novella are going to support a charity collecting money to buy and run an electric wheelchair for a friend's daughter. So it is sort of an acknowledgement that I consider myself extremely fortunate and others don't always have it so lucky.

https://www.justgiving.com/crowdfunding/gill-hardacre

for further information — or if you find yourself with a spare 50p in need of a good home.

As always, thanks to the Tasting Panel readers who passed The Boys of Christmas and made this a possibility: Els E, Isobel J, Elaine R, Yvonne G, Sue R, Cindy T,

Hannah M, Claire W and Isabelle T & Michelle D.

1

'Parcel for you.' There was a clunk and then a heavy weight on my midriff.

'Oh! Sorry, I just closed my eyes for a minute, I wasn't asleep . . . Toby? Why are you here?' I opened my eyes and tried to make it look as though I'd just been thinking deeply, rather than sleeping deeply.

'Father Christmas is off duty, the Milk Tray man couldn't make it and this is my flat and you're on my sofa. Who were you expecting, Daniel Craig?'

Gradually my vision cleared away the blurry dream-memories, and I could see my best friend standing in front of me, wearing a multi-coloured suit, which had juggling balls sewn all over it. 'Well I wasn't expecting Mister Tumble . . . what the hell are you wearing?'

'I've got a kids' party in half an hour. Are you going to open that parcel, or what?' Toby adjusted the most troublesome of his balls, which were hanging from his chest like oversized nipples. 'Better get these tightened up. Nothing like a bunch of four year olds tugging on your décor to make you wish you'd stuck it out auditioning for the Royal Shakespeare Company.'

I stared at the parcel he'd dropped on me. It was a small, square box shape, wrapped in brown paper and addressed with a printed label. 'What do you think it is?'

'Cheap nylon thread,' he replied, still pulling disconsolately at two of the balls. 'If I could work some kind of arrangement where, if the little darlings try to get them off they get a face full of tear gas . . . '

'I don't really think you're cut out to be a children's entertainer.' Poor Toby. He'd had such high hopes after he finished his Drama degree, and so far he'd got two voice-overs and the psychotically cheerful persona of Professor Pat-a-Cake. 'Maybe you should open it.'

He looked at me sharply. Or as sharply as one can be looked at by a man wearing clashing colours and a set of pom-poms. 'Mattie, you should do this. It's addressed to you, look.' He picked up the package and waggled it under my nose. 'It's fine. You're here, you're free. You're allowed.'

'But.' I swallowed and felt sourness at the back of my throat. Months of terror and conditioning, rising up to make my hands weak. 'What if it's from — you know, *him*?'

Toby sighed and sat on my feet, like a spaniel. 'Matz, he doesn't know you're here, I promise. Come on, look, I'll help.' He pulled at a corner of the brown paper wrapping and revealed corrugated cardboard inside. 'Maybe it's an early Christmas present?'

'Who from?' I kept my hands away from the parcel, just in case, and let him keep dragging at the paper until the contents were revealed. 'It's just a box.'

'And a letter.' Toby pulled a much folded and unnaturally heavy piece of paper out from under the brown wooden box, and my hands were suddenly shaky and sweaty. *He's found me. He knows I'm here* . . . Two emotions rose up and fought it out in the region of my heart — one was the urge to phone him, tell him I was wrong, of course I was, he'd been right all along, I couldn't manage without him. I *was* too stupid and plain, too bad with money, too lacking in style to make it alone in the world, and I was so sorry I'd even thought about leaving him.

The other urge was to run. Although where I'd run *to*, given that Toby was pretty much the only friend I had who'd stuck with me throughout my relationship and I was already cluttering his living room, was a question I didn't want to think about.

Toby nudged my elbow. 'Hey,' he said gently. 'You're safe. You're out. Now, open this letter and let's find out who is sending you what looks like a tiny pair of shoes.' He nodded towards the box which, yes, did look like a small shoe box, only one made of black polished wood. 'Come on, there's only so much suspense I can take in this suit before I start to look like a rainbow that's exploded.'

Slowly and cautiously I unfolded the sheet of paper. It was, in fact, two sheets, one folded inside the other, and the first was a headed sheet from a solicitors somewhere in Dorset.

Dear Ms Arden

Your late great-aunt bequeathed the contents of this package to you in her recent will. If you have any further questions about the bequest, please do not hesitate to be in touch.

Yours sincerely
D A H Weldenfield
Solicitor

I stared up at Toby, whose suit was beginning to make my vision flicker at the edges. 'How did he know I was here?'

'Now now, don't be sexist, Matz. D Weldenfield might be a woman. Deborah, I think. Tall and willowy and wears suits from Marks and Spencer's and very practical shoes.' Toby pulled off the jester's cap and ran a hand through his over-long, blond curls.

I knew displacement activity when I saw it. 'Who did you tell I was here?' I jumped up off the sofa with a considerable amount of static electricity accompanying my fleecy pyjamas. I could have illuminated a small city. 'Toby? *Who?*'

'It's fine. Honestly. Just your parents, that's all. They'll have passed it on to good old D A H if you were named in the will, but they won't tell anyone else.' He pushed at my shoulders until I sat down, limp and defeated.

'You don't know *him*. He'll worm his way round my mum, he does this whole 'flattery' thing, 'gosh, Amanda, you're looking younger every time I see you! And so *slim* . . . how do you do it?'' I put on a high-pitched sing-song voice. It was how he sounded now, in my head, whenever I dreamed of his voice. A kind of wheedling, Dickensian-miser type of tone. It helped. ''And I *really* need to know where Matilda is, just to return some of her things.'' I turned my mouth down into 'comic sad clown'. ''I know our relationship is over, it's so sad, but if she wants to leave me it's up to her . . . '' I gave the last four words a sinister spin. And then I started to cry.

Toby moved closer on the sofa and put an arm around me. I tried not to flinch, but I know I did, I felt his hurt withdrawal and heard him pumping his voice full of unnatural cheeriness as he pulled the rest of the package out from where it was wedging itself between the cushions. 'Okay, well, look, here's the rest of it, have a look at this other note, see what that says!' Actually, maybe he wasn't so badly suited to children's

entertainment. His tone was so relent-
lessly jovial it could have raised a
corpse.

Taped to the top of the other sheet of
paper was a small Yale key. I unpeeled it
and read the letter.

Dere Matilda

I am leeving my hows to you. All
you mus do to get this is to scater my
ashes over the boys of Christmas, in
memury of my lost love.

Yors
Millicent Arden-Wynne
St Clere's
Christmas Steepleton
Dorset.

It meant nothing. I stared at the
words until they bled into the paper,
became grey smudges against the white
of the Basildon Bond, the shaky
handwriting and the weird spellings
nothing more than spiders' footprints.

'What?' Toby said.

I shook my head. 'It's my great-aunt

Millie, I think. Dad's aunt. I only met her a couple of times, when we went on holiday to Cornwall when I was tiny, we stopped over . . . ' I tailed off, memory full of a wispy figure of a woman, white hair, nylon trousers and a robust smell of cat. 'And just the once about ten years ago when my cousin got married. She was lovely. Millie, I mean, not my cousin.'

'Slightly, er, erratic spelling.' Toby pulled a face over the note. 'Dyslexic?'

'Dad said she was just 'different'. Never allowed to go to school, her mother taught her to read and write and I think her mum might have been a bit, well, *phonetic* about it.'

'And she's left you a house.' He took the note from me and turned it over. There was nothing on the back, but the deep impression of the letters on the front. Great-aunt Millie had leaned quite hard on her pen to write this. 'In Dorset, of all places.'

'If I scatter her ashes . . . ' It slowly dawned on me what must be in the box and I put it down, carefully, on the floor. 'Over the boys of Christmas? What the hell is she talking about, and is it even legal?'

Toby flicked a pom-pom out of the way. 'It beats lying around on my sofa. As a mission, I mean, obviously you're totally welcome to stay here as long as you need,' he added quickly, and looked at the floor. 'I mean, I'm not exactly throbbing with friendship groups and invites to parties, am I? Not that I want you here just for the company, Matz, or your shepherd's pie. Or to have someone to watch *Daredevil* with.'

I actually managed a smile. 'You need a girlfriend. And you're not going to get one with me slopping around on your FLOPBOT, or whatever IKEA named this thing.' I slapped the cushion.

He kept his eyes on the floor, but a touch of colour tinted his cheekbones. It clashed appallingly with the puce and violet stripes in his suit. 'Yeah,' he said, indistinctly. 'Maybe.' Then he gave his head a shake, causing bauble-ripples

10

across his shoulders. 'Okay, when do we leave?'

I felt the panic hit my bloodstream. 'Leave? What? Where am I going?' Adrenaline sang in my ears for a moment — *I can't go out there. What if he's waiting? He's got my money, my car keys, most of my things; he could have tracked me down . . .*

'Matz.' Toby's voice was calm and steady, the perfect antidote to the fear-rush. 'It's the twenty-first of December. Scatter those ashes — you could be in your new house by the New Year, two hundred miles from — well, from him. New Year, new start, new house, new . . . well, you need new everything, don't you? So, I repeat, when do we leave? I'm presuming that these boys, whoever they are, live in Christmas Steepleton? So, we go there, find the boys, throw a box full of your great-aunt at them, job's a good 'un. You get a house, I get my sofa back, everyone's happy.' He sighed. 'But first, I have to go and twist balloons at eleven four-year-olds, okay?'

After he'd left, I sat, turning the key between my fingers, staring at the note, trying, and failing to remember any more about Great-aunt Millie. I hadn't seen her for more than twenty years and the six-year-old me had been more into appearance than personality, so it was hardly surprising that she existed now as a sort of hook-shape topped with a grey perm and bottomed with trousers covered in tufts of fur. Presumably she'd kept cats, because the only other explanation was that she'd been a werewolf. In the end, and swallowing my nerves, I rang my mother.

'Oh, *there* you are!' she said, as though she could see me through my mobile. 'Yes, Dad's Aunt Millie. She was always very fond of you, and she didn't really have many other people she could have left the place to. Your father wouldn't thank her for it, I mean, *Dorset*, that's practically in France, and he'd never get to work on time.'

Dad was a teacher in a school in Ealing, so she was right. In some ways. In others, of course, she was completely and utterly wrong, but she largely left infallibility to my father.

'So.' Her tone had gone very careful, so I knew what was coming next. 'Have you spoken to Vane lately?'

'Simon, mother. His name is Simon.' He used his surname to introduce himself, because it made him sound more 'exclusive'. Like Morrissey. I used to think it made him different to the other men I'd known, edgy, exciting. What it *actually* made him was a complete knob, with pretensions, and I'd been far too slow to grasp that for my own safety. 'No, I don't want to speak to *Simon*.'

'He's very worried about you.' There was a note in my mother's voice, just the tiniest hint of something, I wasn't sure what but not of the censure I was expecting — she'd thought my moving in with Simon was a huge step up for me, with his fabulous London flat. She didn't know what went on in that flat, when nobody was around. 'He said he thought you'd had some kind of breakdown.'

I bit my lip. She didn't know. How *could* she know, when both he and I had presented a face to the world of a devoted couple, happily in love and always together. *Always*. 'I'm fine.'

'You're staying with Toby? Such a nice boy . . . always so, well, *flamboyant*, but lovely manners.' Mother-code for 'obviously gay.'

'Yes. But Mum . . . ' I tailed off trying to frame the words properly. To put them in a way that she, married to Dad for thirty years with, as she put it 'never a cross word' — although I remembered quite a few very annoyed sentences — would understand. 'Please, please don't tell Simon where I am. I haven't had a breakdown, I just can't be with him any more.' It occurred to me that Simon, sitting in that huge flat with my car keys and money, would know that I had to be at Toby's or with my parents — where else would I have gone? And that he was just giving me chance to 'come to my senses' before turning up at the front door, all forgiving smiles, open arms and those pointed little remarks designed to hurt whilst looking like concern. Dorset was a nice long way away from his brand of sane madness.

'If you think that's best, I'm sure you're right.' Exactly what she always said to Dad when she thought he was being 'highly-strung', although anyone less highly-strung than my father would be clinically dead. 'Anyway, I'd better go, let me know how you get on.' And she was gone. Taking with her that tone of voice that had almost, *almost* sounded like sympathy. Maybe Simon had slipped up somewhere? Let just a hint of the real man slip through that façade of urbane, successful property developer, and shown the hideous reality that lay underneath? It wouldn't be totally out of character for him to have lost his temper when he couldn't find me, to have started off all reasonable and 'I'm so afraid that Matilda might harm herself, she's not stable, not functioning very well' and ended up as the spittle-flecked, puce-faced rager that I had become used to seeing more and more often.

I really hoped he'd let it slip in front of my mother. If memories of my teenage years were anything to go by, she was very efficient in dealing with out-of-control temper tantrums. She might even have set her small but incredibly barky terrier on him and the thought of Simon running with a dog nipping at his trouser legs while he tried to keep his image intact, made me laugh properly for the first time in a while.

2

We drove down to Dorset the next day. The weather in London had been grey and depressing when we left, the streets shiny with showers, and the decorated trees in lighted windows looking strangely unseasonal. Unilluminated lanterns and enormous plastic Santas swayed over our heads in the gusty wind in every town we drove through, but there was no 'feeling' of Christmas in the air. It was too damp and dreary.

I used to love Christmas, when I'd lived at home. Being an only child meant that I'd had far more time, attention and money poured all over me than was really concomitant with being a balanced human being. It had meant that I'd almost come to *expect* a degree of feeling that the universe revolved around me, and a sudden chill pricked down my spine as I stared out of the window at a small Hampshire town. *I'd been easy pickings for someone like Simon. Taken in by his love-bombing at the start of our relationship, because I'd believed, somewhere in my core, that it was just what I deserved.* We'd met at a designer's exhibition, I was there trawling for ideas and he was there because . . . actually, I had no idea why Simon had gone. To be seen, maybe. We'd got talking over a large texture piece, sat and drank champagne and he'd been — oh, he'd been everything I thought I wanted. Charming, handsome, funny, clever. And cruel. I'd thought his sharp remarks and sarcastic comments were just showing off at first. As though he wanted to make an impression on me. Last Christmas had been our first together, and he'd bought me diamonds. The chill intensified as I remembered the New Year party that had followed, and the slow revelation of Simon's true character.

'*Why aren't you wearing that necklace I bought you?*'

'Well, it's a bit posh for a drinks party, isn't it? What if I lose it?'

A tightening of the mouth. An expression on that beautiful, sculpted face that I'd never seen before. 'Wear it.'

'Simon, I'm afraid that it might get broken . . . '

'WEAR IT!'

And then I'd gradually started to realise that the cruelty had been what Simon was really like, underneath. That the gloss and the charm were the disguise he wore to hide the ugly truth about the person he was inside. But sometimes, just *sometimes* the funny, clever Simon would manifest, and everything would be like it had been at the beginning; I'd feel so *loved*. And if only I could keep him happy all the time, not upset him, then he'd always be the Simon I'd first met, the man who'd swept me off my feet and promised me the world. Or, at least, that small part of it that he could control . . .

'You okay, Matz? I can turn the heating up a bit if you want.' Toby wasn't even looking at me, he was concentrating on the road, gilded with frost, that unspooled under our wheels. We were somewhere in the New Forest I thought, the dead brown hands of bracken snatching at the sides of the car as we passed. All these miles and Simon was still with me.

'I was just . . . thinking.'

'Yeah, I could see you 'thinking'. It's over, you know that. You saw him for what he was and you got out.'

I shook my head and went back to looking at the view. Those sporadic trees looked pretty much as I felt inside, endlessly reaching out for nothing, a superficial gloss of passing cold making them look shiny, but underneath they were dull. Pretending to be alive. How could I ever make Toby understand? Yes, I'd got away from Simon, but now I was beginning to wonder how many of the things he'd said hadn't been motivated by his urge to control me, but had been *right*? I wasn't making much of my life. All that training, apprenticing myself to a leading interior designer . . . and where had it got me? Living on someone's sofa.

'So, what else do you remember about this place we're being sucked towards?' Toby flicked the steering wheel around a badger, marching its way along the side of the road like a disgruntled coffee-table. 'You've got to admit, Matz, it's like being squeezed down a toothpaste tube, travelling these roads. By the time we get to Dorset they're going to be two millimetres wide and we'll have to turn sideways.'

The vision of Simon in my head flickered and went out as though I'd turned him off. Real life and Simon weren't compatible. 'Not much, really. Big grey house, nice garden . . . lots of cats.'

'Wow. Retentive memory.'

'Shut up. I was more interested in my *Twinkle*.'

21

Toby started sniggering. 'And another entry for Euphemism Corner! What the hell, apart from the obvious, was your twinkle?'

I gave him a hard stare, but inside my teenage self was giggling filthily. It was a good feeling. 'It was a girls' comic, and should someone quite so euphemistically inclined really be allowed to be a children's entertainer?'

'Oh, come on, after ten rounds of Pass the Parcel and a veritable menagerie of balloon animals, you look for your fun where you can. I once got an hour of giggles out of a cake that was supposed to be a mushroom but looked exactly like a bum.'

My inner teenager was rolling around on the floor slapping her thigh and howling hysterically. My outer twenty-six-year-old had pursed her lips and was trying for a hard stare.

'You're laughing behind that po-face, aren't you?' Toby wiggled his eyebrows. 'Come on, you're allowed to laugh now, Mister 'only smile at high-brow jokes about philosophers and quantum phys-ics' isn't here any more.'

I shrugged and Toby sighed. 'One day. One day you're going to go back to being the Mattie I know, and all that shit will just be a bad dream, you know that?'

'I hope so.' *Trees. Dead inside but pretending to be alive. Everything brown and grey and little flecks of ice.*

'Yeah.' His voice sounded a little less determined now. 'So do I.' Then an elbow nudged me. 'So go on. Give us a smile.'

I bared my lips in a pretend grin.

'Good grief. I've known five-year-olds be more convincing, and, let me tell you, a room full of unentertained five-year-olds is coming a bleak, and yet not-that-distant, second to being in this car with you.'

My stomach sideways-swooped. 'I'm sorry. I'll try to cheer up, honestly, I'm not unhappy I'm just . . . thinking.'

'For God's sake!'

I jumped and flinched in one

movement, and found myself half-cowering against the door, as far from him as I could get in the confines of the Fiat. 'I'm sorry! I'm happy really, look, I've just inherited a house, why wouldn't I be happy?'

The car slid a little as Toby steered it into a muddy gateway and bumped it to a standstill over a frozen rutted verge. 'Matz . . . ' His voice was gentle now, although he was taking such deep breaths that I could see the fur on the hood of his jacket moving in little ripples. 'You are entitled to be as sad, happy, upset or downright miserable as you like. I know you've . . . I know that he has tried to beat all the joy and spontaneity out of you, and it's looking like he's done a good job. I'm sorry if I'm coming over as some kind of CBBC presenter on a truly heroic amount of drugs, but I'm trying, in my feeble and rather toddler-orientated way, to get back the Matz I used to know. I know I'm clumsy and dealing with someone who's been through what you have isn't really my forte, because you're over four feet tall and you don't laugh like a drain when I mention farts . . . ' He spread his hands on the steering wheel. 'I just want you to feel better,' he finished, staring out of the windscreen.

'Me too,' I muttered.

Beyond my window, the outline of that very determined badger wavered into view and clarified, as the single-minded creature caught up with us and, without a single glance our way, veered around us and then continued its trot down the verge. We both watched its progress in silence.

'Sorry I've been *badgering* you,' Toby said. It sounded like the reflexive sort of joke that someone who's spent more time than anyone in the company of small children would make.

'Stoatally all right,' I replied. It took a second, but then he exploded in giggles.

'Knew you were in there somewhere,' he grinned. 'The Mattie I know and . . . well, yeah, knew you hadn't lost it.'

'Lost what? The ability to make really

crap jokes is something I'd quite like to lose, really, in favour of sophistication and cocktail dresses.' I kept looking out of the window as he restarted the engine and the car slithered back out of the mud, clods clattering and clacking off the bodywork as we drove onto the road. My expression, reflected back at me, looked a little softer, backed now by rolling fields and frosty fenced acres.

'I've known you a lot longer than him, don't forget,' Toby said. 'I know the *real* Matilda Arden, the you that you are underneath. And I . . . well, I like *that* you far more than the version he tried to turn you into, y'know? The Matz that I had the epic snowball fight with, the one that fell asleep during horror film night after eating all my popcorn . . . ' He turned his head to look at me quickly. 'Before you got your hair all . . . ' A jittery hand indicated the glossy, hard-to-care-for curls that Simon had insisted looked better on me than my previous, slightly wayward style. 'When you could still laugh.'

We drove through another small town. Here there was less wind and the hanging decorations looked more fitting to the season now that they weren't spiralling about above the streets, but were wreathed in frost in a far more Christmassy way. A large conifer stood in a cobbled square, dotted with lights and surrounded by the stalls of a Christmas market, crowded with people wearing thick coats and ornamented with knitwear. It almost felt as though Christmas was creeping up on us with every mile we drove.

We saw the first sign for Christmas Steepleton as we passed through Bridport, and we followed the satnav directions down roads that got narrower and hills that got steeper, under tunnels of bare branches that joined over the roof of the car. I'd forgotten just how far from main-street civilisation the village was. Or maybe I'd never noticed, sitting there on the back seat of the car, surrounded by boiled sweets and comics and looking forward to our family holiday in Cornwall. The stop-off to visit an aged relative hardly registered, apart from the fact that mum and dad would always break into a whispered argument in the front about whether we should have turned off half a mile back. But we always got there, and the sun had always been shining, and I'd never appreciated that the village was little more than a marker for how much land had slumped into the sea recently.

We crested a final hill, and I pointed. 'That's Christmas Steepleton.'

In the rapidly gathering dark the place was visible only as a series of lights, which seemed to have been stuck on to a cliff face overlooking a blackness of sea.

'Any blue plaques to H. P. Love-craft?'

'What?'

'It's a bit . . . isolated isn't it? The sort of place where creatures from the deep creep into town at night and take all the virgins?'

I gave him a stern look. 'The average age in Christmas Steepleton is about eighty. Any 'creatures from the deep' would be battered and served with chips before they knew what hit them. Anyway. Turn down here, I think.' Vague memories from childhood were surfacing, of the narrow lane that curved gently downhill towards the lights, familiarity gradually seeping in. We passed first one house, then another, lights glowing gently through uncurtained windows into the early dusk. 'This is it.'

Toby stopped the car. '*This* is your aunt's house?' He wound down the window, letting in a sharp gasp of winter air, and stared.

'What were you expecting?' I took in the complete view, a detached house above us set back slightly from the road up a precipitous and complicated series of steps. The walls shone rain-polished and the low gables made the place look as though it was frowning. 'Herds of wildebeest?' Below us stretched the steep, dark, slippery-shiny street, empty of people, which led towards the little cove where I remembered buying ice creams and paddling among rock pools. Behind the house an expanse of garden ran up to the chalk hills, which loomed bulkily above the small town like gym muscles out of a too-tight shirt.

'Something more homely for a start.' Toby adjusted the heater. 'This is like a horror film set. I can practically hear the organ music.'

'Well, it's now *my* horror film set, so we should go in.' I hesitated a moment. 'I mean, if you want to.'

Toby sighed. 'You're doing it again, Matz. I'm not him. You don't have to ask my permission, you know. If I don't want to do something then I'll tell you and we can work it out, not . . . well, whatever it was he did.'

I hesitated with the car door half open. 'He wouldn't speak to me,' I said, voice low, almost as though Simon was hunching down in the back seat about to leap up and contradict me. 'He'd pretend I didn't exist until I apologised and then did what he wanted.'

'Matz.'

'And you know something? He thought he was pretty great because he didn't *actually* hit me. I deserved it, he'd tell me that, all the time, if he'd been a different kind of bloke I'd be all bruises and cigarette burns because I was so crap and so disloyal and so shit at being a girlfriend, but because he was *such a nice man* he was correcting me without hurting me.' The words stopped, although the thoughts and memories that ran them kept going inside my head, overwound clockwork that wouldn't — *couldn't* — stop.

'Yes.'

Toby's agreement jolted me. A smatter of rain that was half-water, half-ice sluiced through the partly open door and stung my skin. 'What do you mean?'

He shook his head for a moment, the

car's interior light giving his fair hair a tinge of yellow, almost as though he was still in costume. 'I mean, yes. Yes, you need to tell me all this, you need to get it out in the open. Your relationship with him was like some kind of infection, Matz, if you keep all the poison inside you it will kill you. You have nothing to feel ashamed of. And . . . ' He stopped, coughed, fiddled with the car keys and wound up the window, appearing almost guilty, then finally looked at me. His eyes were too dark to read in that weak light. 'And I'm glad you feel you can say it to me.'

'We need to go in. It's cold out here.'

Without another word, he got out of the car, and locked it. 'Right. Better get on with it then. You go first, if there's a bloody great tentacled thing in there it's your responsibility.'

We climbed the steps, which were slightly too high for comfort and too steep for safety, and arrived at the forbiddingly dark front door. 'I think my aunt was more cats than Cthulhu,' I said, weakly, hauling the little Yale key out of my pocket. 'And the house is only mine if I can scatter those ashes in the right place. I don't know what happens if I don't.'

'Maybe it goes to the cats' home.' Toby followed me inside, sniffing slightly. 'Although, it smells like it might already have gone.'

The cavernous hallway, with its dark wooden floor, brown painted walls and closed doors leading off it, did have a distinct whiff of territorial tom cat. 'I'm guessing it looks better by daylight.' I'd instinctively lowered my voice. 'It's bigger than I remember, but we usually stayed out in the garden when we visited.'

'Camping?' Toby was cautiously preceding me into the house, keeping one hand against a wall as though he expected them to start closing in around us at any second. 'Or self-protection?'

'We only stopped off to say hello, we never stayed over.'

'Very wise.' His words echoed back to me as he vanished into the gloom, there was a sudden click and a light flickered on, illuminating the point at which the hallway opened out into an impressive staircase. 'That's . . . well, I was going to say 'better', but it really isn't, is it? I'm half expecting maniacal laughter from upstairs any moment now.'

We both listened for a second, but there was no sound other than that of another sleety shower hitting glass behind one of the closed doors. 'It's just a house,' I said firmly. 'All houses feel weird when no-one has lived in them for a while.'

There was an increase in the sound of ice pellets on a window, the light above us flickered and went out, and I let out a squeak. 'It's not the *living* in that worries me.' Toby pulled out his car keys, which apparently had one of those tiny torches attached, because a pathetic beam of light resulted. 'It's more the *dying* thing.'

I pushed at one of the doors and it

opened surprisingly easily, showing the outlines of hibernating furniture under dust sheets. 'Even if my great-aunt did die in the house, she's not still going to be here,' I said, more sternly than I felt. 'It's against the law. Anyway, I know they buried her because mum and dad went to the funeral. I wasn't allowed to go, Simon said . . . ' I stopped.

Toby let the needle of light play over the shrouded chairs without comment. Eventually he said, 'If a talking dog comes through that door, I am leaving. This is a spooky janitor situation if ever I saw one.'

'Shut up.' I nudged him and the light swung around, randomly illuminating more dark walls with pictures on, and a lampshade hanging from the ceiling with an outline that made it look as though a flamingo had landed upside down. 'I can't get used to there not being any cats. If I live here, I'd like to have a cat.'

'It needs something to fill the space out a bit.' We closed the door to that room and I followed Toby down the long hallway to a kitchen, which lay at the back of the house behind the staircase. 'Plus, early warning system for ghosts. I didn't know you liked cats, Matz. And that sounds like the beginning of a Doctor Seuss book, sorry.'

We stood in the high-ceilinged room, all the kitchen fittings were just looming shapes crouched around the walls in the needle-thin torch beam. 'I always wanted a pet. But Simon said . . . ' I stopped. 'Is that an old-fashioned range?'

'That or a coffin.' Toby approached the huge black object that lay against the far wall. 'Anyway, in here it isn't 'old-fashioned', it's practically cutting edge compared to the rest of the room and the term 'cutting edge' probably meant flint tools when this was built. This place gives spooky old houses a bad name.'

We stood in silence for a moment. The quiet was absolute. No traffic passed, not even an atmospheric owl hooted, and the cold was almost solid. 'We'd better find bedrooms.'

Cautiously we crept up the staircase, further into the darkness. A carpet muffled our footsteps and let out a smell of cat and dust as we made it up to the dark corridor of the landing, more closed doors leading off. I opened the first one to reveal a double room with a large iron bedstead, devoid of mattress, and an isolated bookcase. The thin light of Toby's key-ring torch showed that Aunt M had been a devoted follower of Dan Brown and Catherine Cookson, and a rabid collector of cat ornaments.

The next room had two single beds, with mattresses and covers. 'Okay, I'll have this one, you have the double?' Toby said, turning the torch to reveal the swirling pattern of the carpet in fragments, like some terrible hallucinogenic nightmare.

'That sounds . . . ' The door to the double room slammed suddenly in an unfelt draught and I jumped so hard that I nearly knocked him over. 'Actually . . . '

We looked at each other for a moment through the darkness. 'Don't take this the wrong way,' he said at last, 'but I'd feel a lot better if we shared. Just for tonight. And then, supposing all my prayers are answered, tomorrow we can get those ashes scattered and then the place is all your problem.'

I cleared my throat. 'I think that sounds very sensible, actually. I mean . . . '

' . . . strange house, might get up in the night and fall down the stairs . . . '

' . . . so it would be good to have company.'

Moving together, as though we'd been joined by the ankles, but really joined by the terror of being left alone in the big, dark house, we went out to the car and fetched in the sleeping bags, spreading them on the two single beds, then lay side by side in the thick darkness, with the cold scratching at us.

'This isn't what I imagined, you

know.' Toby's voice drifted through the night to me. 'I thought, you know, Dorset, rolling hills and beaches, little cottages. And reliable electricity supplies, wireless connections, heating, all that stuff.'

I pulled my sleeping bag further up towards my nose. The cold had a kind of damp quality to it, and the word 'seeping' kept creeping into my mind. 'It's December. Nowhere looks its best in December.'

Another pause. Then I heard him turn to face me, although I didn't know why, it was so dark that I could barely see him as an outline, backlit by the faintly grey sky visible outside the window. 'Have you ever wondered,' he began, his voice as carefully blank as the glass, 'why Simon let you stay in touch with me? When he stopped you even going to see your parents unless he went too?'

My eyes focused firmly on the ceiling. A pattern of cracks networked across it, as though the roof had been in on the planning of the London Underground. 'I . . . well . . . '

'I mean, I know he wouldn't let you come to the flat, but he'd let you meet me for coffee . . . ' Toby's voice trailed off into a moment of silence that the cold claimed as its own. Bedsprings jangled. 'He didn't, did he?' There was a new note in his words now. 'You met up with me without him knowing, didn't you, Matz?'

How did I explain? How could I make him see? 'I've known you for so long, I *know* you weren't any of the things he tried to make me think you were, I *know* you'd never try to poison my mind against him or force me to leave him . . . he said I didn't need any of my so-called friends, that they were all laughing about me behind my back because they were *jealous*, but I *knew* you'd never be like that! So I . . . ' I gave a shrug that let a slice of cold air slip between me and the sleeping bag, as though the idea of Simon had come along with my speaking about him.

'And that's why you never came to the flat? Why we always had to meet in public places?' Toby's voice sounded surprisingly serious for a man who rarely went two minutes without a pun or a joke. It sounded deeper too, almost as if the weight of darkness was pressing on it and squeezing the 'light-hearted entertainer' out of him.

'I wanted to be able to tell Simon we'd met by accident. In case . . . if he'd followed me.'

'And did he?' Now there was an unmistakable hardness to his tone. The words had been knapped like stone to have sharp edges.

I breathed. *It's Toby. He's not angry with you, he's never been angry with you . . .* 'Once or twice. But never when I met you, only when I went shopping, once when I had to go to the doctor's.'

'He followed you to the doctor's.' A flat statement.

'I'd hurt my leg. Thought I might have broken my ankle at one point, it was stupid, I'd been painting a shelf and I fell . . . '

'And he not only made you go to the doctor alone, but *he followed you to make sure that's where you were going?*'

I could almost see the ripples in the darkness, as those heavy words hit it. Words that felt as though they'd been snapped off a much longer conversation.

'Don't be angry with me, Toby, please. I know it was wrong, I knew then it was wrong, I just . . . '

'It's still not you I'm angry with.' Then he gave a long sigh. 'I wish you could see yourself as I see you,' he said, enigmatically, and lapsed into silence. I bounced around a bit, trying to get comfortable, as another splatter of sleet hit the window, and the closed door rattled on its old-fashioned latch in the gusty breeze which was getting in somewhere and hurtling around the house like an under-exercised Jack Russell.

Toby and I had met at university, both of us creative and up for any challenge — him, as long as it didn't involve heights and me . . . well. That sense of being 'special', the centre of the universe had persisted much longer with me than it should have, and it had taken a good few terms and some serious mental and physical confrontations before I'd been able to accept that there was nothing out of the ordinary about me. I'd just had parents who'd wanted to believe that there was. And so I'd gone to see Toby in all his productions and he'd come to see my end of year collection and we'd gone our separate ways but stayed in touch.

Why had I stayed in touch with Toby? It was a tough question. Was it because I didn't believe he would ever be involved in all the mocking behind my back that Simon said my other friends were taking part in? Was it because I knew I could tell him anything and he wouldn't either assume I was making it up — attention-seeking, or, and almost worse in a way, start demanding that I leave Simon immediately? Because I knew Toby would quietly accept what I said and wait for me to reach my own decisions in my own time?

I finally fell asleep to the sound of the sleet turning into something softer, that blew against the dark windows like feathery kisses.

3

When I woke up, Toby was already downstairs, fiddling about in the kitchen. I put on practically all the clothes I had brought with me, because the house was nose-bitingly cold, and searched him out. The electricity had come back on and he was attempting to boil water in a kettle that looked as though someone had gone half-way to making a cauldron and then chickened out.

'The 1950's called and they want their kitchen back,' he said, waving an arm to indicate an interior that didn't look as though anyone had touched it with a paintbrush since rationing was abolished. 'Actually, make that the 1550's. I brought tea bags and milk with me. I think there are mugs in that cupboard over there.' He nodded towards the pantry. 'I was going to get them but . . . spiders.' A shudder which wasn't over-dramatised. Toby really did have a spider-phobia; he hadn't seen *Lord of the Rings* past Shelob's entrance yet. Poor Toby. I watched him as he dug into his holdall for the promised drinks, lots of theatrical elbows and dramatic sighs all topped with a vast hoodie and blond hair which had formed overnight into tufts and curls. His hatred of creepy-crawlies and his terror of heights combined with his slender frame and gentleness had seen him 'friend-zoned' out of relationships with an almost metronomic regularity. We'd had many a long, late night discussion about why he couldn't find a girlfriend, during which I had regularly reassured him that lots of women like beta-males who might not want to abseil off the Clifton Suspension Bridge or wrestle tarantulas but who were kind, gave ace back rubs and knew the importance of ice cream and chocolate in any balanced diet.

I turned away with a shudder when I realised just how much of a betrayal of all those words my dating Simon had been.

'Okay, mugs, and for your information, no arachnids. Just a load of webs and a collection of dust that would have impressed Quentin Crisp.' I put my head around the pantry door. 'And it's even colder in there, no wonder Aunt Millie didn't bother with a fridge.'

'Plus, you know, big enough for all those bodies, honestly, you could take the doors off this place and use it as a morgue. Perhaps they did. And, even more possibly, still are. Have you checked out all the rooms yet, in case Boris Karloff is lurching around anywhere? It's like *Blair Witch* meets *The Ring*, fights it, and comes up with something even more terrifying. It doesn't even get light!'

I went over to the window and rubbed the glass with the tip of my finger. It was desperately cold. 'That's because it snowed in the night. The snow is all piled up on the window-ledge, look.' I lifted the sash and the window grunted up a grudging half an inch, with a resultant tiny avalanche that cascaded in and covered my socked feet. 'Bugger.'

'Oh, great.' Toby disappeared behind a steam curtain as he poured water on the teabags. 'We get snowed up in the House on the Hill and spend Christmas fending off the army of the undead. I think I saw that film — heads up, it didn't end well for the inhabitants.'

'Don't be stupid.' I tried to brush the snow off my feet. The house was so cold inside that it just sat in little heaps on the tiled kitchen floor, only melting where it was in contact with my skin. 'This is Dorset. You don't get snowed in in Dorset, you're thinking of Dumfries. This is the South West, all English Rivieras and palm trees and . . . ' I wrenched open the big wooden door to the outside, which eventually moved, following a gouged line in the tiling that showed it had always been an effort to open ' . . . Alaskan weather conditions.' Outside, where I knew there should have been a garden riding the rising slope to where bracken and heather took over to the crest of the hill, there was a smooth blanket of snow. The hill itself looked like the nobble of an elbow under a white shirt, jutting into the greyish yellow of the sky. Beyond it, I could see the faint line of hedge that marked the road into Christmas Steepleton, the road itself was invisible under the snow, which looked, even from here, to be too deep to drive through, particularly with the gradient. 'Ah.'

'Well, look on the bright side.' Toby came and stood next to me, surveying the bleak snow-scape. 'Oh no, wait, there isn't one. We're trapped in The Village of the Damned. They'll be able to put us on ice when they've finished with us and keep us til July.'

I snorted a laugh. 'Stop being so overdramatic, Toby.'

He waved an overemphatic arm. 'I

can't! I literally can't! All those children's parties and musical games and primary-coloured clothes have turned me into John Hurt! If the monsters don't get us, I shall emote myself to death.' A comfortable arm rested across my well-padded shoulders. 'Okay, and in other news, what's the plan?'

'Drink tea, dig our way out, find boys of Christmas, scatter ashes, wait for snow to melt and get the hell out of Dodge?'

'Succinct.' The arm gave me a quick hug-that-I-wasn't-sure-was-a-hug-or-just-movement, and Toby went back to the mugs. 'I like it. And what about this house? Put it on the market, in case Hammer Films fancy remaking *The Zombie*?'

I shuffled my socked feet around, taking in the old-fashioned, free-standing kitchen furniture, the dark brown wood of the doors, the collection of flowered china jugs hanging from hooks along the beam above the range.

The cold tinged everything, the air tasted of it, everything I touched felt slick and dead. 'I want to do it up,' I said, surprising myself. 'Turn it back into a proper home.'

Toby curled a lip at me over the edge of his mug. 'With what? Simon took control of your money, didn't he? Shouldn't think there'll be much left, by the time he's finished.'

'I can work, set up a design studio here. It'll be great, actually, I bet loads of these cottages are owned as second homes, people will be lining up to get them made over, come the summer. And I remember how to do interiors on a budget, it's pretty much what I spent my degree doing, after all.' I looked around, imagining the cupboards painted pale grey, the range restored and newly blacked, the tiles polished and gleaming. 'It's a lovely house really.'

'If, as previously stated, you are Boris Karloff.' Toby shivered, theatrically. 'And have the body fat distribution of a yak.' He glanced at the windows. 'It might take ages before we get out of here, this place looks like it hasn't seen the sun since 1977. And aren't your parents going to be missing you if you're not back by Christmas?'

I shrugged. 'They're going to Pamela's, mum's friend. Vane . . . I mean, Simon and I were supposed to be going on a cruise. He'll probably go without me.' A tiny pang dug into my chest, not regret, no, never that, but . . . just a twinge for that part of the life I had given up that had been good. A Christmas cruise to see the northern lights, something I'd always wanted to do. Okay, I would have had to put up with Simon criticising my choice in clothes, my manners, my inability to drink more than two glasses of wine without having to go and lie down afterwards; his silent rages if I spoke up for myself, the two weeks of sulks if I dared go against him . . . I looked around the cold, bleak walls of the old-fashioned kitchen and that twinge died as I thought how much he would hate this place. *Mine*. The northern lights would wait for me. Simon, hopefully, wouldn't.

'Right. If we're going to be here for any length of time we're going to need more teabags.' Toby looked into his cup. 'So if you get out there and start hunting down those boys, I'll make a foray into the local shops, always supposing there *are* shops and not some sort of bartering collective, because I don't think my winning ways with balloon animals are going to get us much more than a ham sandwich.' A pause. 'And now I come to think about it, *that* combination of words is probably never going to come out of my mouth again.'

I changed into some clothing more suitable for venturing outdoors, although, given the temperature, that really just involved putting a coat over the top of what I was already wearing and pulling a woolly hat around my ears and, with Toby making 'shooing' motions as he pushed me out of the front door, I set off out into the snow-covered streets of Christmas Steepleton, with the box of my aunt's ashes deep in my pocket. After all, I never knew when some boys might present themselves, and I might as well be ready.

The steps down to the road were icy and I had to hold on to the bushes in order not to slither down the whole lot. The road itself wasn't much better. It led steeply down to the distant cove and harbour, and was currently filled with snow and lined with houses, like someone had domesticated the Cresta Run. Any cars that were about had clearly been parked since last night, judging by the snow heaped on the roofs and the lack of any tyre tracks.

The sea lay at the bottom, like a dirty blanket, grey and creased with waves, washing against the cliff edge with an impatient hushing sound, overlaid by the petulant cries of gulls. To my left lay the little harbour, where a few fishing boats toddled about, sheltered from the worst of the wave action by a long wall which curved out into the sea and against which it broke in half-arsed curls of spray. To my right was the tiny beach where I'd played while mum and dad had sat with Aunt Millie in the beach hut, reading the paper and performing other, boring adult tasks. The beach huts were gone now, I could see. Where the colourful boxes had once stood was now an expanse of slumped earthy cliff, overgrown with bleached adolescent trees.

I inched my way down the slope, zigging and zagging to avoid picking up speed and schussing embarrassingly past the village and down into the sea. To my surprise, despite the debilitating snowfall, most of the shops that occupied the street, which branched off the hill and ran parallel to the sea, were open. Their lights were a welcome antidote to the bleak snow-scape and the scary dark of Aunt Millie's house, and I went in to the first shop in the row, which looked as though it had been converted from either a lifeboat station or a particularly militant shed.

It was warm inside. Little lanterns hung from a beamed ceiling, shelving was covered in fairy-lights and a Christmas tree stood against one wall. There were posters stuck up everywhere and items which looked handmade scattered across all surfaces. A girl sat behind a sort of counter, knitting, and she looked up, startled, when I came in.

'Thought the road was closed,' she said. 'Did you walk over the cliffs?'

'No, we came down last night. We're staying in Millicent Wynne's house up on the hill.'

The girl looked back down at her knitting. 'Oh, ah. I heard she'd left that place to some niece or something?' She had multi-coloured dreadlocks and was wearing a kind of artistic smock thing that seemed to be mostly pocket, on each fingernail the varnish was a different colour. My eyes ached at the result, but that was partly the shock.

After a night in Millie's sepia-toned house, I would have found a copy of *The Times* a bit too colourful.

'Yes, that's me. I'm Mattie Arden.'

The girl lay the knitting down on the counter. 'Oh yes, I remember you,' she said. As she was at least five years younger than me, and would have been an infant the last time I visited, this made me frown.

'Really?'

She sighed. 'No. But that's the sort of thing people expect round here. I was going to bluff it. So, what can I do for you?' She stood up and I saw she was wearing a name badge that said 'Thea', multi-striped leggings and Doc Marten boots that laced up to her knees. 'There aren't many people who come in on days like these, hence this.' She picked up the knitting. 'By spring I should have a bedspread done.'

I looked around. 'This is nice.' By which I really meant 'this is a pleasant contrast to a house with no heating and intermittent electricity'. The shop was a little bit 'cutesy' for my taste, self-consciously 'seaside holiday gifts' like pastel water-colour paintings of Christmas Steepleton and stones with little homilies like 'Be Peaceful' carved into them.

Thea shrugged. 'Does well in summer. But . . . ' she picked up a hand-painted lighthouse, which was about ten centimetres tall and a carved wooden gull at least twenty five centimetres high, ' . . . scale, people. I have nightmares of being attacked by twenty-foot black-backs. Anyway. What can I do for you?'

It felt a bit weird, launching into my tale of ashes and house bequests, so I wandered around for a minute, looking at the displays. Amid the seaside items were occasional knitted creations, a seascape half woven and half crochet, which was very effective, and some cushions in muted colours which somehow managed to conjure images of sunsets over sea and moonlight on water. 'Did you do these?'

Thea shrugged. 'Yeah, well.' Her

attitude was a mixture of resignation and pride and I picked up one of the cushions, admiring the quality of the stitching and the blending of the colours.

'They're lovely.' Under the cushion I found a knitted octopus, with each leg a different colour, and a big smiley face. Impulsively I picked him up. 'I'll take him. He'll make a great Christmas present for my friend.' Toby could call him Cthulhu. He was probably a bit light on the tentacle front, and way too cheerful to be a demon, but still. 'But please can you gift-wrap him? I didn't bring any paper or anything . . . we only came for a couple of days but it looks as though we're going to be stuck here for Christmas.'

Thea took the octopus and went to the counter. 'We're usually swamped out at Christmas,' she said. 'You'd be amazed how many people want to come to Christmas for Christmas, it's only the weather that's put them off this year, the forecast is bad for the next week or so, and nobody in their right mind wants to get snowed in here. This is a place it's all right to visit, got a naff name that looks cute on postcards, that's all. We've not even got a Sainsbury's.' She carefully didn't look up from cutting paper.

'We never thought to check the forecast,' I said, a bit chastened by her assumption.

'You're from . . . London?' I nodded. 'Shouldn't think weather forecasts mean much to you up there. Bit of wind, bit of rain . . . ' She gave a nod towards the high hills. 'Up there, for the farmers, it can be life or death, so we take notice. Plus, you know, bulk buying fishfingers and everything, cos they don't send the helicopter in until day three.' She stuck down a final piece of tape and handed me the squishy parcel. 'Right. Anything else?'

'Does the phrase, 'the boys of Christmas Steepleton' mean anything to you?' I dropped Cthulhu in my pocket.

She laughed. 'Er, no. Dating potential round here, precisely zero. There's one young guy who does the ice cream stall, but he's like seventeen so practically a baby. Zac and Jed up on the cliff there.' A jerk of the head to indicate the road down which I'd come. 'But you'd be wasting your time there, they've been a couple forever, they are so kidding themselves if they think nobody knows. That's pretty much it for men under fifty.' She bit a fingernail, the turquoise one, thoughtfully. 'There's a boys' school up on the hill, some of the teachers are blokes. I suppose you could give that a go. And some archaeology types digging around on the top of the cliff sometimes.' She looked me up and down. 'If you're desperate.'

I drew myself up, about to take offence, but then I looked down at myself, bulked out in lots of clothing and topped with an old coat and the washed-out feeling that running away from Simon had left me with. 'No, thanks. I'm off men at the moment. But I need to find the boys to scatter my aunt's ashes.' And I told Thea the details of my bequest, while she chewed another nail and then laughed.

'Mad old bat.' But it was said affectionately, and besides, the smell of cat and the house décor didn't really contradict that impression. 'Used to see her wandering up her garden, up to her ankles in cats, but I don't know about any 'boys'. Could ask my gran, I suppose, she knew your aunt Millie.'

'Oh, could you? That would be great.' Visions of two old ladies chatting over tea about long-past lovers, hunched under shawls in rocking chairs were dashed when Thea said, 'Yeah, but I'll have to wait til tonight to ring her — she's in Australia, gone on an adventure holiday.'

I left Thea settling back with her knitting, and went out into the street again. In contrast to the warmth and light of the shop, it seemed dark. The sky was a threatening grey, reflected by the sea's pewter shade. The creamy white breakers that rolled in up over the rocky beach to lie in lacy tatters on the strip of sand, showed up bright in the greyness on one side, and on the other side the lights from the shops shone out onto the snow. The railings that separated the road from the drop down to the beach were woven with Christmas lights and I found myself wondering how they fared when the spray from a rough sea splashed over them. Surely it was irresponsible to have mains-powered lighting somewhere that water could get in?

And then I stopped. Pulled up short by the thought that it wasn't my kind of thinking. That was a very *Simon* sort of thought. I just liked the fact that someone had taken the trouble to tangle coloured lights around a rail, someone cared enough about the appearance of the village and the season to try to brighten things up with lanterns. Maybe they were battery-powered anyway. And Health and

Safety wouldn't let anyone do anything that would be dangerous, would they?

Get out of my head, Simon. I'm tired of thinking what you want me to think. Wearing what you want me to wear, being the person you want me to be. Or allowing myself to be moulded into the sort of person you think you deserve to be with — compliant, quiet, intelligent but not too intelligent. Nothing to challenge your view of the world as conspiring to keep you from making those millions you deserve. The silent, pretty woman in the background, wearing the clothes and jewellery that say nothing about who she is, but are all about how you want to be perceived . . .

I found myself gripping the railings with both hands, as though to stop myself from climbing over and letting myself drop the twenty or so feet down the slowly crumbling cliff that separated the road from the sea. Simon was gone. I'd left, we were over.

I just knew that he wasn't the type to

let me go that easily.

'Hello.' Toby appeared beside me. 'Sea still there then.' An elbow nudged at me. 'Any luck with the boys? Good grief, this whole experience is giving me a set of phrases that I am absolutely *never* going to use again.' He had a bag swinging from his wrist, his hands being deep in the pockets of the fur-hooded duffle coat that made him look like an overgrown five-year-old.

'There's a boys' school further up there.' I pointed towards the top of the hills above the village. 'Apparently. Other than that, and a teenager and two gay blokes, nothing that I can think would remind Aunt Millie of her long lost love.'

'Aha!' Toby reached into the bag. 'There is also . . . this.' He produced a pamphlet. 'In my search for comestibles with which to create some kind of Christmas feast — no real luck, they don't have proper shops here and we were only half an hour away from Christmas dinner being two choc ices and a stick of rock — I found the Tourist Information Office!'

I stared, first at him, where his hair was being pulled from under his hood by the sea wind, teased into a fusilli of spirals and then blown back against his forehead, and then at the pamphlet in his hand. 'They have a Tourist Information in Christmas Steepleton? Who for, a bunch of seagulls down from Hull?'

'Come on, you know it's not always like this! Dorset in summer is heaving with people. This is part of the Jurassic Coast . . . fossils and . . . well, mostly fossils, but fossils are popular. Plus, sea, sand, ice creams, all that.' We looked out for a moment across the heaving sea with its doilies of foam. 'Okay, hard to imagine at the moment, but, yeah. Tourists. So . . . ' He tried to unfold the paper, but it blew and danced and formed new creases and he ended up having to bend it around to show me the relevant part. 'Look.'

It was a small picture of a hillside. Faint lines showed white in the chalk, but that was all I could make out. 'And this is . . . what?' I looked at his face. His greenish-brown eyes were lit up from inside, like the shop windows and there was a little half-grin that kept bursting out on his face.

'This, my dear Matz,' and he put his arm around me again, bundling in close to stop the paper being whipped out of his hand by the nervous little wind that was skirling around us, 'is a picture of an excavation which is going on as we speak, up there.' He pointed with the arm not hugging me, and the pamphlet scrunched itself into a ball around his wrist. 'All right, probably not *literally* as we speak because of the four feet of snow and the minus several million of centigrade, but it's a current excavation. This says . . . ' and he let me go to flatten out the paper against a nearby bin, 'that 'faint chalk marks indicate that figures were once cut into the hillside' . . . blah blah something historical . . . 'appearing to be two small male shapes, currently known as . . . '

wait for it . . . the boys of Christmas!' With a 'ta da!' sort of motion, he flipped the paper into a smaller shape and tucked it back into his pocket. 'Your underwhelment leads me to believe you are less than impressed, Matz,' he said. 'And it's far too close to Christmas — the time of year, not the place although, yes, the place as well — for that kind of expression. Come on, there are boys everywhere!' A moment. 'And, yes, I realise that I should probably be saying that with a *bit* less emphasis.'

Under my feet the snow squeaked and crunched as I stomped my boots to try to get some feeling into my toes. 'I thought this was going to be easy,' I said.

'Nothing is worth having if it's too easy,' Toby said, hunching his shoulders against a new wind. This one came off the sea and held salt and the smell of seaweed, like the waves were breathing out. 'Are you done here? Shall we go back to what I am going to have to call 'the house', purely because it's got walls and a roof and therefore cannot be described as 'the graveyard'?'

I pressed my hands deep into my pockets, feeling the crunch of paper and the soft ball that was the little knitted octopus, and managed a little smile. 'I suppose so. I can come back tomorrow to find out if Thea managed to talk to her gran in Australia.'

'Thea?' Toby began to walk beside me, our feet cracking the snowy surface in a pleasing kind of unison as we picked our way back along the seafront towards the hill leading up to the house. A few, very bundled-looking people were walking about now, none of them looked particularly pleased to be outside, but it stopped the streets from looking quite so *Whistle and I'll Come to You* . . . damn it, now Toby had got me at it, thinking of Christmas Steepleton as some creepy film location.

'She works in there.' I gestured at the little gift shop as we passed. Thea was standing in the window, gazing out across at the sea. She saw us and gave a regal sort of wave, then turned back to her knitting. 'That's Thea.'

'Wow.' Toby stopped walking and turned sideways. 'She looks amazing. What's she like?'

Of course. Of course Toby, with his drama school background and his love of brightly-coloured things, would get on with someone like Thea. Of course he would. I should take him into the shop, introduce him. Walk back to the house alone and leave the two of them to get to know one another, who knew where it might lead?

But I kept walking. 'Didn't really talk long enough to find out. Nice, I think. Her gran knew Aunt Millie.'

He tore himself away from the window and extended his stride to catch up with me, snow flurrying around his legs and making dark splashes up his jeans. 'Okay.' A moment of breathless escalation and then, 'Can we slow down a bit? Only I'm beginning to feel a bit Sherpa.' He held up the carrier bag. 'This is surprisingly heavy for two tins of soup and a loaf of bread.'

His hood had come down, or he'd lowered it to get a better look at Thea, and his hair was flat against his head, which made his eyes look huge. A couple of days' growth of stubble was ornamenting his jaw with blond spikes. 'You're more yeti than Sherpa, I'd have said.' But I stopped anyway. 'Two tins of soup and a loaf of bread? Is that our Christmas dinner, then?'

He leaned forward, getting his breath back. 'No, it's lunch for today. The shop, surprise surprise, does deliveries. The rest of the food is coming later.'

'By husky?' I looked up at the sky. It had taken on a yellowish tinge, the lumps of cloud that hung over the village had feathery edges as though the weather was being airbrushed in. 'I think it's going to snow again.'

'We're not exactly a polar exploration team,' he said. 'I should think they can manage to carry it a few hundred metres up to the house, even if a bit more snow should happen. Anyhow, I think we should get back, light a fire, preferably with all the furniture, and pool our findings. FYI, I also ordered a Christmas tree, so get up in that attic and see if there are any decorations to put on it, will you?'

'Why should I go in the attic?' We started walking again, leaning into the steepness of the hill and occasionally grabbing one another to stop ourselves sliding back down again.

'Your house, your organ-playing-maniac-demon,' he said. 'And I refuse to let Christmas go uncelebrated, just because we are trapped in some Poe-Lovecraftian nightmare, so if your aunt left any baubles around the place, I want them dug out, stat. And if there are any mad old women up there . . . '

' . . . you'll invite them out for a drink,' I finished.

'Exactly. Because only mad old women fancy me these days.'

We reached the bottom of the steps and I looked up at the house in daylight — if you could call this grey snow-potential daylight — for the first time. 'Is it just me, or does the house look ... pleased to see us?' Somehow, maybe it was the reflection of the snow, but the white stone trim around the windows looked brighter, the grey walls less forbidding and the slumped snow on the roof gave the place the look of a building wearing a particularly jaunty hat.

'It's just you.' Toby went past me and started up the steps, dragging himself up with much recourse to bushes and shrubs. 'It's a house, not a Labrador.'

'Maybe it's just because we've opened it up a bit.' There was less of that tang of cat when we opened the front door this time, and because we'd pulled a few curtains back, light spilled in and made the hall look bigger. Less brown. That feeling I'd had in the kitchen last night settled over me again. 'I could do something with this place.'

'Yep, set it on fire and collect the insurance.' Toby went into the kitchen and I heard the definitive sound of soup cans dropped on the big pine table. 'Lentil or pea and ham? Sorry, but it's all they had left.'

'No, I mean . . . do it up, turn it into . . . I don't know, boutique B&B?' I wandered after him and hitched myself up onto the table.

'Er, Matz, you do know that every other building here is a B&B, don't you?' He emptied the two tins into saucepans and began hunting for a way to turn the gas on. 'You'd have to do something really special to make it different, and I'm still voting for the blowtorch option.'

I stared past him, past the old-fashioned gas cooker and the inert range, out through the window that gave a view of the steep slope of garden. It was a white sheet, the occasional hummocks of perennial plants making it look like a giant scoop of ice cream, but I could see the potential there. A summer house, for guests to sit out on warm evenings, this room, repainted and modernised but with a lot of the old-fashioned features kept in. Flowered tea services and cake stands and full-length curtains. ' . . . so I think that could be our next move. Matz?'

'Sorry,' I gasped out the apology before I remembered I didn't need to do this any more. This was Toby, not Simon. Toby who knew me, who understood me, who didn't expect instant obedience. 'Sorry,' I said again, but genuinely this time, not reflexively. 'I was thinking about how this place could look.'

Toby left the saucepans on the stove and came over to look into my face. 'You're really caught up on this, aren't you?' he asked, quietly. 'You sure it's not just something to escape into? You know, occupy your mind now you're not with Simon?' There was an expression in his greeny-gold eyes that I couldn't read. 'Are you really that desperate to get away from London?'

'I don't know.' I fiddled with the bevelled edge of the table. 'Half of me thinks that I shouldn't let him drive me away, but the rest just wants a new start. Somewhere different, somewhere I can make something for myself, a little business, without having to worry about Simon bloody Vane popping out of the woodwork every fortnight to remind me how pathetic I am and how little my life is amounting to without him in it.'

Toby followed my stare and started looking out of the window too. 'More snow,' he said. Huge, feathery flakes were falling, like an immense number of sky-ducks moulting at once. 'I hope that shopping delivery turns up otherwise it's all going to get a bit *Lord of the Flies* in here.' He took a breath. 'You do realise that it's only your self-belief he took, don't you? Nothing else. You're still as good at everything as you were before you met him, you're still the same person, Matz. *He* tried to make you into someone else, someone he could push around and mould to fit whatever it was he wanted from a girlfriend — but that was all *his* problem, not yours.' A wide arm thrown out to encompass the whole house. 'You can do anything you want! You always could! You want this to be the best B&B in Christmas Steepleton, then you go for it girl . . . ' Now he was back in front of me. 'Make it happen,' he said, his voice suddenly lower and fiercer. 'Make it happen, Mattie.'

His faith in me was like the antidote to Simon's perpetual negativity. As I watched the steam curl up from the heating pans of soup, I could feel this new life solidifying around me. *This* house. *My* life. Nothing to do with what had gone before. I could do it. I felt a kind of rising joy inside me, anticipation and optimism mingled with a feeling of freedom that I didn't have to return to London, I could stay here in Christmas Steepleton forever.

Well. 'As long as I can get these ashes scattered over the boys. The house won't really be mine until I do that.'

'Who'd know? I'd tell everyone that those ashes got scattered good and proper.'

'The boys would know though, surely. Suppose the solicitor is in touch with them now, and they tell him?'

'Or her.'

'Thank you, or her, that I've not been anywhere near them? And besides, I'd feel all weird. Knowing that I hadn't done what Aunt Millie asked me to, I wouldn't feel that the house was properly *mine*, if you see what I mean.'

Toby sighed and scraped soup into bowls. 'Yes. Yes, I get where you're coming from. And, yes, it would be cheating to tip the ashes out in the garden or wherever. You need to find out about these boys, find out which ones have a connection to your aunt, and, presumably, if they mind having late auntie thrown all over them. *Then* you can start making plans. And I hope ... ' He stopped, suddenly, concentrating very hard on the lumps of pea and ham sliding into the bowl.

'Mmmm?' I broke off a crust from the bread.

'I hope . . . I hope you'll let me visit, now and again. I mean, I'm in on the ground floor, as it were, so I'd like to see how you get on with the place.'

The thought that leaving London would mean leaving Toby hit me suddenly, somewhere the warmth of the soup couldn't reach. Loyal, over-dramatic, colourful Toby, who'd never questioned me, never harried me, just been . . . well, Toby.

'I . . . ' Not being able to just text him and meet up whenever life seemed to be getting a bit too serious would be . . . 'I mean, of course, you can come whenever you like! Maybe . . . maybe you could be the bloke who always has the attic room that nobody else is allowed to book. Like a 1950's film.'

He dropped his face so he was looking into his soup. 'I'll miss you,' he half-mumbled. It was dawning on me how much I would miss him too, but he swallowed the mouthful of pea and ham and changed the subject. 'How old was your aunt? When she died, I mean.'

I dipped bread in the soup. Simon would have ignored me for days if I'd done that in front of him. 'She was Grandad's sister, they were all born around the mid-twenties, so . . . about ninety something, I think.'

'So.' He scraped the bowl with his spoon to get the last of the soup up. 'We don't know when she wrote the letter leaving the house to you, do we? Anyone who might have been a boy when she wrote it could be an adult by now. I mean, even if she wrote it ten years ago, they'd still not be classed as a 'boy', would they?'

'Oh, great.' I dipped more bread, enjoying the freedom to do it more than the resulting soggy mass. 'So you're saying we need to round up all the males in Christmas Steepleton and throw ashes at them? That's going to take some organising.'

'Not as much as you'd think. The lady in the food shop told me there's only about fifty permanent residents, and practically all of them either run shops or the B&Bs. You could say it's some kind of local Board of Trade meeting . . . And if half the inhabitants are female, you're only looking at about twenty, twenty-five people. You could practically hold it in a shed.' He looked around the kitchen. 'Or in here. Which is pretty much only not a shed because it's got curtains.'

'You're mad.'

'Hey, Professor Pat-a-Cake here only one juggling ball away from certification.' He ran water onto his bowl. 'Okay then, Buffy, what's your plan?'

'Well, I was thinking I could ring the solicitor. Find out when the instructions were given, that would give us a time frame to work from, except, it's Christmas week, and the solicitor will be at home, not in the office, so that's not much use. But I'm thinking that Aunt Millie would have known that she could live quite a long life, if she gave that letter to the solicitor any time between the last time I saw her, when I was about sixteen, at my cousin's wedding, and she must have done it after that or she would have just given it straight to me or at least told me about it . . . ' Toby was watching me with his head on one side. 'What?'

'Nothing. It's just nice to see you coming back.' I gave him a stern frown and he leaned back against the sink, with a grin. 'You're losing him, Matz. Gradually, but it's good to hear you with a bit of oomph about you again. Anyway. You were saying?'

'So. Aunt Millie must have known that anyone who was a boy when she wrote that note wouldn't be a boy by the time I got it. Which means . . . '

' . . . that it's something that is a permanent boy. We're looking at those chalk figures then, up on the hillside?'

'Got it in one, Sherlock.'

There was a knock on the door and Toby leapt into the hallway. 'That'll be the delivery. No, don't come, I . . . there's a Christmas present for you in there and I don't want you to see it. Get up into that attic and wrestle the mad wife for possession of any tree decorations that might be up there, right? And don't come down until I say.'

'Bloody hell, what have you got me?'

'A werewolf. I want to make sure he's chained up before you come in.' Toby shooed me up the staircase before he opened the front door to a white curtain of falling snow and a vague shape beyond.

On the upstairs landing I gazed upwards, failing to see the expected hatch in the ceiling, so I walked along opening doors in case it was in one of the bedrooms. Nothing in the double room, nothing in the room Toby and I had shared. The chilly little bathroom with the high-level cistern and the claw-footed bath had nothing more interesting than damp stains on the ceiling, and the other two rooms were completely empty, except for some dusty piles of books. At the end of the landing another door revealed a bare set of stairs leading up, and, only slightly daunted by Toby's certainty that there was something spooky about the house, I left it open as I ascended.

I'd half hoped that the attic would be full of piles of letters, old diaries, clues as to what I was supposed to be doing, but although Aunt Millie clearly hadn't been keen on interior decorating, she'd been queen of minimalism. The attic contained some more piles of books and a few cardboard boxes, all carefully labelled in Millie's slightly eccentric hand. 'Old Cloths', which, when opened, held dusty dresses, a few shabby looking coats and some battered shoes, the promisingly labelled 'Payprs', which proved to be nothing more than stacks of ancient newspaper, dusty and stacked into the box haphazardly. I picked one out, but it was ancient, yellow and blurry, obviously awaiting use as packing material or insulation. The final box bore the legend 'Decerashuns', and revealed that Millie had all the decorating style of a magpie that had seen one too many editions of *Kirsty's Handmade Christmas*.

I picked up the box and headed back downstairs. From the landing I called, 'Is it safe yet?'

'Just chaining him up now.' Toby emerged from the front room. 'But I wouldn't go in there, if I were you.' He shut the door carefully behind him. 'I thought we'd put the tree up in the kitchen. That being practically the only room without the Addams Family vibe.' He led me into the kitchen, where a tree that must have stood three feet tall in its high heels, was propped against the table. 'Apparently this was the only one they had left. When the snow came in the entire village had to go to the local shop for Christmas supplies.'

The tree leaned among a pile of newly shed needles. To call it 'threadbare' was to do battered teddies everywhere a disservice, it looked as though it had been spat out by a hurricane. The contrast to last Christmas, the six-foot tree hung with crystal, the expensively wrapped gifts among the branches, the sense of luxury about it all . . . I laughed, and that, too, was a complete contrast to last Christmas. 'It looks like we should have it adopted.' I produced the box of 'decerashuns'. 'And here's what we have to hang on it.'

'Blimey, looks like a milkman crawled in there and died.' Toby produced something made of tinfoil bottle tops. 'And, in this house, that is not an unreasonable supposition.'

We propped the tree up in an old jug, held upright with bags of sugar and began festooning it with items from the box. These were mostly home-made; apart from the foil creations there were painted fir cones and some inexpertly knitted things that might have been intended to be stocking-shaped but were twisted and holey so they looked more like worn out socks. At the bottom of the box was another, smaller box. Pale cream, it looked as though it had never been opened. 'What's this . . . oh.'

I pulled open the flap lid with difficulty. Inside, amid a mass of soft tissue paper was the most exquisite little glass ball. I took it out and held it up. It was painted with old-fashioned lettering in gold, and had a tiny Father Christmas near the base.

'Baby's first Christmas,' I read the lettering. 'Oh God.'

4

Toby picked up the box and looked at it. 'It's old,' he said. 'Look. There's a price on the bottom, seven shillings and sixpence. Pre-decimalisation, so before . . . what, 1970?'

'And it was still sealed. I had to break the tape with my fingernail.' I realised why the box had been so hard to open. 'Oh, Toby, do you think . . . ?'

It twisted from an untied loop. 'This was never hung, so whatever happened, there was never a baby in this house.' Toby reverently placed the bauble back in its box.

'Well, technically there were, all my grandad's family were born here. This was their family home, Great-aunt Millie was the last one left living in it.'

Toby didn't make the obvious joke about there not being much living about this house. He just looked at the little white box sitting on the table. 'I think your great-aunt Millie thought there was going to be a baby,' he said, softly.

We both looked at the box in silence for a moment, then I picked it up and put it away in the bigger box, with the spare decorations. There was a new chill in the kitchen now. The cold that comes with cheated expectations and thwarted wishes. 'I wish I hadn't seen that,' I said at last. 'It makes it all real. Up to now it was just inheriting a house from an old lady I hadn't seen for ten years, now it's . . . she was a real person. Her lost love . . . ' I choked off.

'Okay.' Toby took a deep breath. 'Okay. We can't unsee it — along with some other horrible sights, like the lampshade in the living room — so we use it, yes?'

'How?'

'Well, we know she was thinking about a baby, and they, contrary to what you might have been told, don't get brought by storks. If she knew a baby was likely, or was even pregnant, then her 'lost love' was someone she was sleeping with. We're not dealing with some man she had a vague crush on from afar, it was a real relationship, so someone, somewhere in this place must know who he was. So, we can get corroboration that the 'boys' she is on about, really are those shapes up in the chalk.' He gently took the big box and put it out of sight, under the table. 'Because you don't want to go off half-cocked, scatter the ashes up there and then discover that, actually, Millie had been having a fling with a teacher up at the school and wanted her mortal remains chucked around during an assembly, do you?'

'You're really quite a sensible person, aren't you, Toby?' I wiped the moisture that had collected in the corner of my eyes with a sleeve.

'Yup. That multi-coloured costume of mine covers a body full of practicality and pragmatism.' He indicated his chest, which was currently covered by an Aran sweater and a body-warmer. 'Also not nearly full enough of food. Come and help me put away the stuff I got for Christmas dinner. Although, given how cold it is in here, we can probably just leave it on the side.'

'We don't want the werewolf to get at it though.' I picked up some of the various bags of foodstuffs scattered around the counter. 'And I hope you got sprouts.'

'Oddly enough, there were lots of those left.' Toby came to help. 'Christmas dinner this year is mostly green.'

We pushed things into various cupboards and the pantry. I watched Toby, in his massively over-sized sweater, competently sorting food into 'meat, veg, fruit and — other stuff'. 'So, what were your plans for Christmas this year?'

He didn't even look up. 'Try to barge in on another family having dinner, then sit at home watching the *Doctor Who* special with a couple of cans of cider.'

'No, I was being serious. What were you supposed to be doing that you've had to cancel to sit it out here with me?'

He rolled his sleeves up to his elbows. 'I was being serious, Matz,' he said. 'You were loved up with Simon the Vane, Mum lives in Portugal with some bloke whose name I can't pronounce, my sister would spend the whole time telling me I should get a proper job — hey, heads up, Cassie, children's entertaining *is* a proper job, okay, it's not *EastEnders* but it pays — and that's pretty much it. There's a few friends I can go to for lunch but I'm not up for gatecrashing a full day, besides, I always end up minding the kids and it's a bit of a busman's holiday, to be honest.' He looked around the kitchen, which now seemed a lot more homely, with the tree decorated and a couple of bags of satsumas which we'd dropped into a bowl in the middle of the table. Snow flurried outside the windows, but somehow the room felt warmer — although that could have been the soup. 'This, and I hate to say it because it makes me look pretty pathetic, is an improvement.'

I went up to him and gave his shoulder a squeeze. 'Sorry,' I said softly. 'Sorry that I never even asked you to come to Christmas dinner.'

He snorted, and there was a hint of bitterness. 'What, and watch you do all the cooking and waiting on the table of our Lord Vane, like a cross between a housemaid and his own, private sex toy? Uh uh, Matz. I wouldn't have come if you'd asked me. Not to see you like that.' And then, with a more normal tone, 'Besides, he wouldn't have let you invite me, would he? He wanted you all to himself, so there was nobody to tell you how outrageously badly he was treating you.'

'*You* told me, though. Every time we met up, you told me he wasn't right.' My hand was still on his shoulder, although he was wearing so many clothes I would have had to perform a mining procedure to have reached Toby underneath.

'Yeah. And now I know that we were meeting furtively — ever wonder why he didn't want you to be around any of your friends?' He raised his eyebrows at me. 'Because he knew they'd always tell you the truth, that's why. He took you in, Matz, but the rest of us . . . we knew what he was like, we could see what he was doing to you.' The eyebrows furrowed. 'We could see the real him, the him you'd been blinded to.' And now his voice softened. 'The him that you would have thrown out of the house if he'd let you see. I'm an actor, Mattie. I know how it's done.'

More silence. More snow falling.

'So you don't think I'm stupid? For falling for it? Even though you could see what he was like and I couldn't?' My voice sounded very small. And those greenish-brown eyes were very big, shining, reflecting the snow, the gently rotating silver milk bottle tops hanging from the sad tree branches.

'You,' he said softly, 'couldn't be stupid with special exercises.'

The moment stretched into the silence as though time was a sheet of elastic around us, and we weren't staring at each other for ages but for a millisecond snipped out of a lifetime. Then there was a loud bump and crash from the front room, and Toby pulled away. 'Bloody werewolf must have slipped the restraints,' he said and went out, closing the door behind him.

I leaned back against the table, making the Christmas tree rock. *Toby.* Looking at me as though I mattered, as though I were special. Was that what he thought? Was *that* what it really was between us? I held my breath when I heard him come back in, but he was brisk now, that few seconds of something else had been flushed out by the draught of the open door. 'Right. So. What? We . . . go up on the hill? Take a look at the 'boys'?'

Suddenly I felt reluctant to leave the

house. This sparse kitchen with the feeble tree felt as though it was the centre of something huge and if I went outside — well. The feeling might disperse, hit with snow and air and the reality of life. And then I told myself how idiotic that was, and if I didn't make some kind of inroads into finding these boys, then the house wouldn't be mine and I'd have to go back to real life anyway. 'Okay,' I said. 'I'll just go and find a duvet to put on or something.'

'It will be fine when we're moving.' It almost sounded as though Toby wanted to be out there, with fresh air and sanity. 'At least, I'm hoping so. I can't feel my fingers already, so it's not like it can get much worse.'

'That has to rank alongside 'I'm going outside, I may be some time', as snow-related understatements go.' I began struggling back into my boots. Crusted snow still stood along the soles, very gradually melting into little rivulets on the tiled floor of the kitchen.

Booted and coated, we stood at the

front door. The snow was falling more slowly, as though the clouds had got lazy now they'd driven everyone back indoors, and we tumbled our way down the steps to the road amid clearing visibility.

'Why is it always bloody uphill in this place?' Toby grumbled. 'I feel like we should be roped together.' The snow was deeper in pockets where it had blown and collected, against walls, against cars parked on the precarious slope, but in other places it barely covered the road. By trying to keep to these patches of windswept tarmac we managed to haul ourselves up to where a Footpath sign pointed the way across a plain of whiteness towards a distant disturbance of the horizon. 'That must be the archaeology dig thing that they're doing. Shall we head for that?'

I caught my breath. 'In the absence of any other landmarks, I'd say yes.'

We struggled our way along the top of the hill, through snow that reached past our knees. There was a faint, trodden path in the snow already, and paw-prints, where someone must have been along with a dog, but otherwise it was as smooth as a high thread-count sheet on a new mattress. We plonked along in silence, the effort of walking keeping us warm as the snow burned our feet with the cold and the wind tried to take our noses off.

Eventually we reached what turned out to be a couple of tents and a large marquee covering bare soil. 'Look at that view,' Toby said, almost wonderingly, his breath puffing out in little squiggles as he spoke. I turned to see the snowfield tufted by trees and hedge-tops stretching down to the outlying buildings of the village. Beyond the buildings we could see the curve of the harbour wall embracing the little cove, and the beach on the other side, on which silver waves were breaking gently, into unheard curls of surf. A string of coloured lights marked the railings between the shops and the sliding cliff edge and a rising row of cloud showed the horizon. 'Apart from the lack of heating, decent shops, access roads and mobile phone reception, who would want to live anywhere else?'

'Try us,' said a voice, and we turned to see a bundle of clothes climbing out of one of the tents.

'Sorry, we didn't think anyone would be here.' I clambered closer through the snow. 'We've come up from the village.'

Another face peered out through the tent flap. 'Well we didn't think you'd parachuted in.'

'How many of you *are* there?' Toby asked curiously. 'Is that tent like a clown car or something?'

A deep sigh. 'It's just me and Patrick. The others had the sense to get out when the snow was forecast, we were going to wait it out and go in the morning.' There was a beard under the multi-layered hats and scarves. '*He* said it would blow through.'

'You're archaeologists, right?' I watched the second bearded figure clamber out of the tent. 'How long have you been up here?'

'Four million years,' said the one who wasn't Patrick. 'That's how it feels when you're in a tent in a snowstorm. You haven't got a flask or anything, have you? I'm gagging for a cup of tea.'

'There are boys *everywhere*,' Toby said, sounding happy, and the one that was Patrick coughed.

'Oi, you haven't even bought me dinner yet, don't jump to conclusions.'

I suggested that we all went back to the house, for the archaeologists to have a cup of something hot and, after having been in close proximity to them for a few minutes, a wash, and possibly stay over until the snow cleared. 'It's okay, we've got loads of room.'

'How do we know you're not a pair of serial killers?' asked the one who wasn't Patrick, but was, in fact, called Kieran.

'Because *she* is an interior designer and *I* am a children's entertainer called Professor Pat-a-Cake, and any two people less likely to turn to serial killing you are not likely to find. Although, actually, after a particularly tricky party with a difficult crowd, I have been tempted to lay about me with a balloon poodle.' Toby led the way back, retracing our footsteps to try to limit the amount of snow falling into our boots.

'And I don't take criticism well,' I said. 'So, you know, opinions to yourselves, chaps.'

We trailed back to the house and clambered up the icy steps. When I opened the front door and Toby said, 'By the way, nobody goes into that front room, right?' I sensed a certain hesitation on the archaeological front.

'You are absolutely *sure* you aren't serial killers?' Kieran stamped snow off his boots on the doorstep. I wanted to tell him it was a waste of time, but didn't like to. 'Only, I know martial arts, and Patrick has a devastating line in sarcastic put-downs, so I wouldn't tangle with us, if I were you.'

'But they are serial killers who are offering us cups of hot tea,' Patrick mitigated. 'So I say, let's go with it and take them down if they try anything, okay?'

We went through into the kitchen and I watched the archaeologists start taking their coats off, get a hint of the internal temperature of the room and decide against it. Kieran took one look at our Christmas tree and pulled a face. 'I take it back. Serial killers have style.'

'We might be trainee serial killers.' I put the kettle on, and the two lads focused on it in a way that told me it had been a long time since they'd had a hot drink. 'But we aren't. We really want to ask you about your dig.'

'Ah, ulterior motives coming out now.' Patrick peeled off his knitted hat, to reveal ginger hair. 'Okay, ask away.' He hoiked himself up onto one of the stools that dotted the kitchen like punctuation marks. 'Only, nothing too academic, we're only second year students.'

I looked across at Toby. I couldn't think of anything to say, now I was confronted by a sort of reality. 'How long has the dig been going on?' he asked.

The lads looked at each other, as though for corroboration. 'Four . . . five years? Something like that. Uni's been sending student groups here for at least the last two years, we came last summer.'

'And when did the figures start to show up?'

Kieran scratched his beard. 'I know this one. There's always been one figure up there, everyone called it the Man on the Hill. Then, one year, someone discovered that there was something else carved in the slope, there were crop marks. So they sent a team out and that dig established there had once been two figures, side by side. We're looking for dating evidence, y'see. They seem to be stylised outlines, something like the Gemini figures in some Roman . . . '

'So, people have only known there

were *two* figures quite recently?' Toby gave me a significant look.

'Yeah, something like that. Doesn't seem to have been a folk-memory in the village either.' Patrick ran a hand through his hair. 'Any chance of a bath?'

I poured mugs of tea whilst Toby hunted for a switch for the immersion heater that we'd already established stood concealed in the bathroom in a cupboard big enough to house a horse. When the men had gone upstairs to establish a base camp in one of the empty rooms and to unload their rucksacks, Toby slumped down on the edge of the table. 'So. Maybe it's not those boys then.'

'Aren't you enjoying this just a bit too much?' I put the now empty tea cups in the sink and started to run hot water. The sudden scream from upstairs told me that this had caused some kind of sudden cold water influx into the bath.

'It's a bit like a detective story

though, isn't it? Come on, Matz, you can't say that it isn't interesting, can you? You stand to gain this whole house if we can solve the puzzle! And, let's face it, your aunt must have intended it to be like this otherwise she'd just have told you exactly where to scatter her ashes, none of this 'boys' thing.'

'Unless . . . ' I said slowly, 'it was some kind of shameful secret. Like she couldn't even bring herself to write it down.'

'You're thinking of that decoration, aren't you?' Toby's voice was quiet. Almost calm. 'That baby that never was.'

I looked up. At the ceiling, with its faint tracery of lines, the pale, institutional green walls, at the old furniture and ancient cupboards, the web-festooned pantry. 'This house must hold so much history. So many memories,' I said. The little Christmas tree wobbled slightly as I walked towards it, the uneven floorboards creaking. 'And not all of them will be good.'

Outside the window the dark was gathering. Almost knocking against the glass, trying to get in but held at bay by a fifty-watt bulb. 'So, what? We owe it to your aunt to find out what happened?'

'It's not just about the boys any more. I mean, yes, we still need to find out where to scatter those ashes, and the sooner the better because we can't just camp out in this place forever, can we? You need to get back for work and I need . . . I need to sort out what I'm going to do with the rest of my life. But I want to know about . . . about what happened.'

Toby made a sort of 'wrist shrugging' motion, opening his hands. 'You realise we might never find out,' he said. 'There's already so many candidates, just for the ashes, almost like your aunt *wanted* it to be complicated.'

'Maybe she didn't though. Maybe, when she wrote that letter, there were no other candidates, maybe it was simple and straightforward *then*. Maybe it's only just got complicated.'

And I looked at him when I said it, willing him to see down through the layers of words. *It's complicated.*

'But if it was simple, would it be worth anything?' He had his eyebrows raised in a sort of 'comedy rueful' gesture. 'Isn't anything worth having worth a bit of complication?'

Another moment of silence, this time broken by the clamour of footsteps as a socked archaeologist burst into the room. 'Bloody hell!' It was Kieran. 'I just realised, tomorrow is Christmas Eve! Anyone got a working mobile, I have to ring my fiancée or I am as buggered as a completely buggered thing.'

Toby handed over his phone and we tried to ignore the sounds of Kieran being shouted at down the line for several minutes.

'So, we've eliminated those boys . . . ' I said, quietly, under the sound of someone trying to apologise for meteorological intervention. ' What next?'

'There's still the school. And the

male content of the village,' Toby whispered back.

'Well, there's not going to be anybody at the school now, is there? It'll be the holidays.'

'There might be someone, a care-taker or something, who might know about your aunt. I reckon we should go up there tomorrow.' He looked down at the floor. 'Before trench foot settles in permanently.'

'And what are we going to do about . . . ?' I jerked my head towards Kieran, still frantically apologising.

'They followed us home, can't we keep them? No, really, Matz, we can't let them spend Christmas freezing in a tent, can we? We'll just have to spread the Christmas food a little bit.' Toby grinned. 'Come on, you can't say you've ever spent a Christmas like this before, can you?'

At which point Patrick burst in. He'd got half a beard. 'I was trying to have a shave, but I think the sink is blocked,' he said.

'I can honestly say that I have never had *anything* like this before, let alone at Christmas.'

5

Toby and I shared the double room again. Patrick and Kieran took one of the empty rooms and, once we'd finished trying to work out some kind of bathroom routine, we all settled down into our sleeping bags. Outside, a deep silence had fallen, as though not even the local wildlife wanted to be about, not so much as an owl hooting or a cat yowling broke the blanket of quiet.

I was lying in my sleeping bag in a onesie, a fleece and three pairs of socks. Toby had a big hat with ear flaps on. 'You'll have to put in heating and some more bathrooms,' he said, when I finally got settled. 'Unless you're running a 1940's themed boarding house.'

'I know. But it can be done though. Can't it?' I was aware I sounded a bit pathetic, but this relentless cold was getting to me.

He turned to face me. His hat, unfortunately, didn't revolve with him, and he ended up talking into one of the ear flaps. 'Course it can. If anyone can do it, it's you, Matz.' A moment of quiet, in which we could hear Kieran, whose own phone was now charged, talking, presumably trying to convince his fiancée that he wasn't spending Christmas surrounded by gorgeous women in some kind of seraglio. 'So. Tomorrow we hike up to the school, yes?'

'But it's Christmas Eve!'

'So? Life still has to go on, whatever particular religious festival may be taking place. It's Hanukkah too, by the way, just so you know, but you never hear people saying 'oh, let's not disturb them, it's Hanukkah', do you?'

'Okay, you win. We'll go up to the boys' school. And I also have to go down to the village. Thea said she'd ring her gran tonight and see what she had to say on the subject of Aunt Millie.'

'And we probably ought to get in some more sprouts,' Toby said, thoughtfully. 'Those boys put away the last of that loaf like they hadn't seen solid food for a week. Although sprouts aren't really a foodstuff, they're more an excuse for additional gravy.'

I pulled my sleeping bag up to my nose and closed my eyes. I wondered what Simon would say if he knew where I was now, although I knew what he would have been doing if he'd been here. He'd have been spending all his time on the phone to estate agents, finding out how much the house was worth, he wouldn't have cared a damn about making sure the ashes were scattered properly. In fact, he'd probably have pulled the box from my hand and thrown them into the garden. I could almost see his face, that expensively cut blond hair damp under the snow and the sneer on his lips as he stamped the ashes into the earth under a bush. 'There. Sorted. Now let's get this place sold.'

And he'd have made me believe that it was the right thing to do. Made me think that there was no way I could keep the house, that the money would be better spent in any one of a hundred ways — most of which would benefit him. And deep in my heart I would have known it was wrong, might even have tried to say something, but he would have talked over me, given me that look, the one that said 'I can hear you talking but all your words are stupid and meaningless', told me that he knew what he was doing and someone with as little sense and practicality as me shouldn't question him.

And I would have believed him. Because he knew exactly how to play to my insecurities. How to pick up and build on every doubt I had, every fear, every shred of uncertainty, twist it and turn it and make it true. I fell asleep to dream uneasy dreams of silence and oppression and hopelessness and bitter, biting cold.

The next day the house felt even more homely. The kitchen was full of people doing busy things, Kieran was making toast on the gas grill, and Patrick and Toby were arguing over a bowl of cereal about the best way to heat beans. I put the kettle on and felt the house relaxing around me. This must have been what it was like in its heyday, when my great-grandparents had a houseful of children. My grandfather had been one of six, two boys and four girls, and the girls had all been educated at home, so the place must have been in constant bustle, with a couple of maids dashing around after the family, a gardener to help keep the stretch of hill in order . . . I could almost see the kitchen as it would have been then, the deep sink with a mangle clamped to it, a clothes airer above the range, a copper for boiling clothes. And then my smile died as I remembered Aunt Millie as

I'd known her. No-nonsense, but in a slightly ethereal way, as though her memories were fragile and might be blown away at any minute. How had she been able to live on here, when all her siblings were gone, and her hopes for her future lost? What had it been like for her, rattling around alone in the place, with only her cats for company? I wished I'd taken more time to get to know her. Visited more, stayed here and listened to her stories of growing up in the middle of that big, chaotic family, with a father hardly around and a mother who insisted there was no need for girls to go to school. How had she felt about that? And, when her sisters had all married 'suitable' young men, how had it been for her, staying at home as nurse and companion to her increasingly frail mother? Had she fretted against the confines of an upbringing that expected the unmarried daughters to live at home until they died? Or had it been comforting to know that she might have lost her love, but she would have a home forever?

'What are you frowning at?' Toby asked through a mouthful of cereal. 'You look like you've got rampant indigestion.'

'Just thinking. The house feels different with lots of people in it.'

'Warmer, for a start.' He scooped the last of the milk up. 'As long as we all huddle together in here, like penguins.'

'Do you want me to . . . errr . . . attend to that matter?' Patrick was giving Toby meaningful looks. 'You know, that . . . matter . . . ?' He jerked his head towards the front room.

'Oh, yes, right, if you would. While we're out.' Toby started pulling on his fur-hooded coat.

'The werewolf?' I asked.

'Yeah, that. If you could just . . . you know, feed it, walk it, keep all silver bullets to a minimum, that kind of thing?'

Patrick nodded, seriously. 'Least we can do. You letting us bunk in here has saved us from having to squat in that tent and eat cold camping food for Christmas, so, reckon we can help you out.'

'And I'll go down to the shops while you're away.' Kieran clearly didn't want to be thought of as a freeloader. 'Get some more food in.'

Toby pulled a face. 'Reckon by now they'll be down to Pot Noodle and sprouts, but, knock yourself out. Or, don't, we don't want medical emergencies as well. If this was a book, one of you would be about to give birth about now.'

The archaeologists looked at one another. 'Bags not me,' Kieran said. 'I'd be rubbish at labour. I don't even vote for them.'

'I'd take one for the team.' Patrick shrugged. 'But, you know, not going to happen.'

'Okay then. In the spirit of continuing the 'sentences I am never going to say again', if neither of you can manage to have a baby while we're gone, I'll be grateful. Come on, Matz, we've got a hike ahead of us and only one packet of bourbon creams to assist us because *someone* had night hunger.'

'Sorry.' Patrick didn't sound sorry at all. 'But I've been snowed up in a tent for two days without biscuits of any kind. Leaving them lying around was just cruelty.'

I shrugged myself into my coat, pushed my feet into my still-wet Wellington interiors and followed Toby out of the front door. The journey down the ice-coated steps was beginning to feel easier, now my hands knew which bushes I could get a grip on, and it was with the minimum of comedy slipping over incidents that we arrived on the road. Last night's snow had filled in all the footprints we'd left yesterday and laid another inch on top of the previous depths, so now as we trudged upwards we sank to our thighs through a crusted surface.

'It's like walking through icing,' Toby said. 'Don't you think? Really deep icing. Like on top of a Christmas cake deep. Not that rubbishy thin stuff you get on lemon drizzle, that's barely icing at all, it's more like a sugar wash.'

'Are you really hungry or something?' I reached out for a hand to pull me up the last bit of incline.

'Yep. Really, really hungry. And now all I can think of is cake.' Toby's hand was warm, even though he wasn't wearing gloves. 'And Christmas pudding. And brandy butter . . . Do you know how to make brandy butter, Matz?'

'Nope.' This high up the snow had frozen into a solid surface that we could stand on top of, but it was treacherously slippery. 'And even if I did, I doubt the shop will have any brandy, from the sounds of it.' I kept hold of Toby's hand as we trudged on. 'We should have brought the werewolf, we could have harnessed it to something and used it like a sled-dog. How much further?'

' 'nother couple of miles I think.' He

stopped again and looked around. Everything gleamed, it hurt my eyes. Even though the sky was a heavy grey colour, the snow glistened and glinted in what light there was, giving the hillside a polished look. We were walking along a lane at the very top of the hill that became the cliffs above Christmas Steepleton, high hedges had sheltered the road from the worst of the snow so we no longer sank quite so deeply in, but the crunching noise was getting on my nerves. 'Look, there's the sign.'

A big, posh-looking road sign, covered in half-drifted snow stuck up out of the hedge. Toby went and dusted it off. ''St Dabney's Pre-Preparatory School for Boys, 4–6 years,'' he read. 'Poor little buggers, being sent away from home to live out here.'

'Oh, I don't know. Look at the view,' I said, perching on a gate in the hedge. Being right up here meant we couldn't see Christmas Steepleton, it was tucked into the linen folds of the cliff below us, but we could see the wide bay mouth, the striations of different rock formations as the coastline stretched towards the distant horizon, the freckles of white water on the choppy sea and a small boat that must have sailed from the harbour and was heading further out.

'Yeah, because if there's one thing a four-year-old boy likes more than his home and parents, it's a good view. Come on, Matz, you're not telling me you'd send your son out here! Even for a top notch education.'

'Of course not.' I bridled at his sarcastic tone. 'My dad teaches at an academy, I'm practically programmed to find private schools elitist and divisive. But, you know, each to their own.'

He joined me up on the gate, warm and bulky beside me. 'I know.' His breath formed little clouds and hung around his stubbled cheeks in beads of water. 'Bet Simon will be sending his kids away somewhere like this.'

It sounded a bit like a challenge. Almost as though Toby was testing me. 'I think he'd have wet nurses lined up for straight after birth,' I said, evenly. 'He wouldn't want the mother of his child to be soiled by anything as demeaning as having to actually feed her own baby.'

Toby snorted a laugh that billowed out to join the cumulus forming overhead. 'It's good now you can see him for what he was, Matz.'

'He wasn't all bad.' I kept staring out over the far-away sea.

'Oh, do tell. No, wait a minute, he didn't beat you to death or shut you in a cupboard to starve to death? What a prince among men.'

'Shut up. No, some of the things he said about me, like me being wishy-washy about my career . . . you know what? He was right. I am, *was* 'wishy-washy' about it, because now I'm realising that it wasn't my thing, not what I should have been doing. *That* is why I think I'd like to run a

B&B, it's not just some idle whim. Not some 'oh, I've inherited a house and I don't have a clue what to do with it', but truly, really, something I think I can do, that I can be good at.' I glanced across at his face, hoping his expression would tell me what he was thinking, but it was impassive. As blank and chilly as the snowfields that surrounded us.

'You,' he said, and his tone was level, 'have never been wishy-washy in your life. You don't even know the meaning of the word. Words. But if you want to think that bastard did you a favour then, go ahead, believe it, but *you*, Mattie Arden . . . ' and now he was standing very close, the clouds of our breathing mingling to puff away in the cold air, 'you are fucking perfect.' A pause, in which another man might have kissed me but Toby just stood, eyes on the far horizon, then wheeled like a gull on the wind. 'Okay. Let's get to this school and ask whether your aunt had anything to do with any boys. Only, let's not phrase it like that, all right?' And he was leading the way, marching along following the pointing arrow from the school's sign, until the hedges broke away from us and we were walking up a wide driveway towards a building that gave the house in the village a run for its money in the 'spooky' stakes. It even had a tower, for god's sake.

6

A large sign above the door told us to ring the bell and wait for an answer, so we pressed the button and waited.

'This place must never meet your aunt's house,' Toby said. 'They might mate and have really scary little bungalows.'

An intercom voice told us that the school was closed for Christmas. I explained that I just wanted some information and, after a short, cross-purposes conversation during which the voice kept asking me to check the school's website, we were buzzed inside.

'Ah.' Toby took a deep breath. 'I'm glad to know that private schools smell exactly like state schools. Old dinners and feet.'

We were met by a man who introduced himself as Head of the

Lower House, which made me wonder how on earth you could have a Lower and an Upper House when the children concerned were between four and six years old, and shown into an office, where we sat in unaccustomed warmth, and I asked about my aunt.

'Millicent Arden-Wynne . . . name isn't familiar.' A computer, then a filing cabinet, then a Rolodex were all consulted, but all, apparently, came up blank.

'No rumours of any affairs among the teachers?' I asked. And he laughed a hollow sort of laugh.

'Miss Arden, have you seen our location? I presume you have, since you walked here from the village. There're no other buildings for two miles, and the nearest pub is at the bottom of Christmas Steepleton main road. Our teachers rarely even leave the premises, of *course* there are affairs, but they are all in-house, so to speak. I'm assured by my junior colleagues that it's either sleep with each other or watch *The Kardashians*.'

Toby leaned forward. 'This would have been a long time ago, maybe the forties?'

Another hollow laugh. 'You might not remember,' said the Head of House, 'but there was a little business of a world war going on then. This place was a training camp for army officers from 1935 to 1950, and from 1950 to 1973 it was an RAF nursing home. We, the school, took it over in 1974.'

We found ourselves back outside in the snow, the memory of central heating and the smell of freshly brewed coffee coming with us like 'what could have beens'.

'So. No boys until 1974. That's post decimalisation, so after everything was over.' I walked down the crunching, tightly packed snow of the driveway, a newly risen wind gusting through my hair.

'What about all those army officers and injured RAF boys? Very dashing, a

man in uniform . . . never mind your
aunt, *I* want one.'

'There wouldn't be any point scatter-
ing her ashes over the boys at the school
if she'd been seeing a military bloke
though, would there?' I pointed out.
'She'd just have asked to have her ashes
scattered somewhere in the building.'

'Or the grounds. I know I never met
her but I've got your aunt down as not
being beyond some rumpy pumpy in
the bushes of a summer evening.'

'Now you are projecting, Toby.'

He sighed. 'Sorry. It's these trousers.
So. Not the chalk figures, not the
school. What are we left with? Someone
from Christmas Steepleton.'

'And it's Christmas Eve, we're
snowed into Dorset with a pair of
archaeologists and no heating.'

'But, bright side and all . . . ' Toby
swept an arm to indicate the view. 'This
is where we're spending Christmas. If
you squint, it's a bit like the Alps.'

'If you close your eyes completely it's
almost like Mauritius,' I said, stamping

my feet. 'Except for the anoraks, the wet wellingtons, the lack of sunshine and the soup.' But he had a point, I had to admit. From the ridge of hill we could see Dorset rolling away like white corrugated card. On the other side lay the great grey heave of sea. Gulls hung over the cliff crying like disappointed cats, but otherwise the air was silent. 'No traffic, that's why it's so nice. Thea said that the place was inundated at Christmas, because of the name, everyone must have cancelled when they saw the weather this year.'

'So, this is our ideal opportunity. No outsiders, just 'the boys of Christmas', perfect timing for us to find out who to scatter these ashes over.' We started walking again. Downhill it wasn't so bad, and we slithered back into the village in time to meet Patrick and Kieran inching their way up the hill to the house.

'We got more food.' Kieran held up a bag. 'Some of the boats went out this morning and there's fresh fish.'

'It's like being marooned on a desert island,' Patrick said, happily. 'A bit.'

The relatively higher indoor temperature and the ability to walk without high stepping like a pony or sliding backwards, made the house a relief. I sat in the small room that might have been a study had Aunt Millie needed to study anything, while the boys bickered lightly in the kitchen about the best way to cook whiting. There was a feeling of 'uncurling' about the house now, as though being lived in was making it less gloomy.

When Toby came in I was doodling designs on a bit of paper. 'Look. If we knock through the front room and kitchen we could have a big, L-shaped space that would be the heart of the house. Keep the range, put a dining table *here* . . . '

'Wouldn't it be better to have two separate rooms? So people can get away from the smell of cooking?'

He asked in a reasonable tone, not dismissive, but it still threw me back through the months. Simon, knocking back any of my suggestions about adapting his flat for us both to have our own separate spaces. 'It's better if we sit together to work,' he said. 'Then I can keep an eye on what you're doing!' Said with a little laugh, a tone that made the words not sound as threatening as they should have. I hadn't picked up on that 'keeping an eye', hadn't realised that it would mean watching my every move, commenting on my stupidity in decision-making, my inability to prioritise. Asking about my texting, my phone calls, following me from room to room to make sure I wasn't calling anyone he didn't approve of. Wasn't escaping . . .

'Yes, of course, you're right,' I said, automatically. *Don't argue, don't justify, it only makes him worse, makes him more insistent. Battering at me with words, with reason, keeping the argument going until I was too tired to think straight, stopping me from sleeping 'because we can't go to bed on* a disagreement', on and on and on until . . .

'But, y'know, it would give the kitchen a better view, front and back.' Toby was watching me carefully. 'So it could work.'

'Yes,' I said eagerly. 'And the sun would be in the room all day, so it would be lovely and bright.'

'Although, this looks like a load bearing wall.' He tapped at the wall behind him. 'So could be risky.'

'Oh well, it's just an idea. What?' He was staring at me now. 'Why are you looking at me like that?'

'You realise you just changed your mind three times in the course of one conversation? To agree with what I was saying?'

I mentally re-ran what we'd said. 'Well, so did you.'

He nodded slowly. 'Yes, but not in response. I was just disagreeing with whatever you said. And you changed your mind to fit in with me.' He came from the doorway to where I was sitting on a beaten-up old armchair that looked as though several determined cats had tried to destroy it. 'He's still in your head, Mattie.'

'He isn't!'

'Yes, he is.' He crouched down in front of me, looking into my face.

'You're right' I slumped. 'He is.'

'Or are you just saying that to agree with me again?'

'Well, if you're going to be like that about it . . . ' Why had I never noticed how long Toby's eyelashes were? Or how his eyes were the colour of that bottle glass that the sea sometimes throws up, polished smooth but with a kind of light of its own, held deep inside? He was pressed against my knees and I could feel him breathing, feel the cushioned firmness of his chest inside the thick sweater. 'How do I get rid of him?'

'I don't know.' His voice had a hoarse tone, as though the words had been dragged out. 'I wish I did, Matz.' He reached out a hand and touched my cheek. 'I wish I could exorcise him. Throw him out of your brain into the hell he deserves.' How were his fingers so warm? I was only a couple of steps away from hypothermia, but Toby was throwing out heat like a blowtorch. 'I wish I could make you forget him.'

'He wasn't all bad. At the beginning he was funny and clever and witty. It made me want to be with him.'

'It's called entrapment. Or hypnotism. He did it on purpose, it was all an act, so you'd give up everything he told you to. Look what he did to you. He took the lovely, confident, artistic Matilda Arden, with all her friends and her hobbies and the things she loved, and he turned her into this shadow girl, afraid to express an opinion or contradict anyone. She gave up her friends, put her family at a distance, stayed in all the time . . . and why? Because some tosser with an expensive haircut and a nice line in persuasive chat told her she wasn't good enough at what she did.' He raised himself up now, so he was level with my face. 'Don't let him win, Matz. Seriously. Don't you *ever* let *anyone*, not him, not me, not even your mother, tell you you're not good enough. Because you are. You are bloody amazing.' His voice gave a little jump, as though it was catching on some of the words. Snagging on the emotion that he was putting into them, and the heat in his eyes was so intense that I had to look away.

'Toby, I . . . '

'Right. Pep talk over.' He jumped to his feet and went to stand at the window. 'Wind's getting up. If you want to talk to Thea at the shop, now might be the time, they'll be closing early on Christmas Eve, won't they?' He was keeping his back to me, every knitted line of the Aran pattern showed a rigidity in his muscles.

'I suppose so . . . ' My indecisiveness even annoyed me. 'Yes, of course. Good idea, I'll go now.'

'That's my girl.' The windowpanes shook as another gust of wind dashed up the hill. 'Do you want me to come?'

Just the fact he was asking. Asking, not telling me he'd get his coat . . . this was Toby, not Simon. 'No, it's fine. You'd better stay here and supervise Patrick and Kieran and those fish, otherwise it's pea and lentil soup again and my stomach is already starting to make 'no, no' noises.'

A pause. 'Okay.' He made a movement as though he was going to turn around or say something else, but then changed his mind and kept staring out of the window. The snow that had previously settled on bushes was being whipped up by the rising breeze and occasionally hitting the glass with a splattering sound like little beads. I could feel the draught from here.

I struggled back into my coat and boots and headed out for the shops. I could hear the sea moving; a great uneasy beast, booming and thrashing as it hit the base of the cliffs. Drifts of spray rose up over the railings as I turned into the road to see the shop lights reassuringly bright, spilling onto the snow which was being gradually eaten away by the tops of the waves that nibbled through between the Christmas lights.

'Oh, you're back.' Thea was knitting again, something two-toned and fluffy.

The inside of the shop smelled of scented candle, of wool and new fabrics. The calm warmth contrasted nicely to the thrashing wild cold outside. 'I just came to ask if you'd spoken to your grandmother. You were going to ring her last night?'

A toss of the dreadlocks. 'I tried, but she'd gone shark fishing. I'll get her tonight though, it's Christmas Eve, and we always talk at Christmas. It's hard getting the timings right though, she's near Melbourne and it's the middle of the night there now.'

I picked up some little woollen figures, feeling let down. Thea's grandmother was pretty much my only hope for any idea of who these 'boys' might be now we'd eliminated the likely candidates. 'Oh. Thank you.' Two of the felted figures looked slightly familiar and I realised that one had red hair and the other had a huge beard, they looked a bit like Kieran and Patrick. 'I'll take these, please. As Christmas presents.'

As Thea wrapped the little men in gift paper, I looked further around the shop. A noticeboard near the door gave details of craft clubs and knitting groups and also appeals for carol singers to gather in the village square at 6 p.m. on Christmas Eve. 'Carol singing?'

'Yes. We go house to house, like detectives with better voices and less agenda.' She stuck tape along seams.

'Does most of the village do it?'

'Oh yes. We go around to all the tourist hotspots, earn a fortune for charity. There's usually more Americans staying, and they love all that 'tradition' stuff.' Outside the sea roared and spat. 'And the weather is usually better. We're going to have a tough time doing 'Silent Night' over that racket. There.'

She handed me the two packages.

'Will you come and sing up at my aunt's house?' It would be a good opportunity to get a look at the 'boys of Christmas' and, besides, I still couldn't really get myself into the Christmas spirit, some carols might be just the thing.

'What, up those steps? In this?' Thea looked towards the shop window. 'It's practically Plague of Frogs out there.'

'I'll put some salt down on the ice, that'll help, won't it?'

She gave a sort of thinking shrug. 'Yeah, the Christmas Steepleton carol singing slugs might be put off, but we'll be fine. Okay, I'll ask.'

'Thank you.' I pocketed the gifts and went back out. The gale was still rising, flecks of sea foam mingling with the snow, like toppings on ice cream, and I struggled my way against the wind back up the hill.

'There are literally no forms of inclement weather left to be thrown at us now,' I said, walking back into the kitchen. It was distinctly warmer in there, the three men were kneeling down in front of the range. 'I admire your dedication to the power of prayer, but . . . '

'Patrick's got it going.' Toby hurried over. 'Means we've got heating and hot water. And also a means of cooking what appears to be the world's tiniest chicken. In fact, I'm not even sure it is a chicken, I think Christmas Steepleton might be one gull short of a picnic-attack.'

'Still better than cold camp food in a tent.' Kieran straightened up from where he'd been fiddling with a valve. 'Even sprouts are better than that.'

There was a sudden glooping noise from the range and Patrick thumped it. 'Grandparents had one of these,' he said. 'The secret is not to show weakness.' Another hearty thump on the metal top and the noise stopped. The temperature was increasing notice-ably. Toby had taken off the sailor's sweater and looked much more normal in his shirt. The archaeologists had got down to T-shirts, but I suppose their blood must have thickened what with camping in snow.

'We're somewhere between Haunted House and Furnaces of Hell,' Toby said. 'Trying to balance out before something explodes.'

I went upstairs to take off some layers. The house felt — well, 'human' now, for want of a better word. Lived in. There was noise downstairs as the men congratulated one another on getting the range working, the pipes were ticking and clicking as they warmed up, and the rooms no longer felt like freezer cabinets. Although outside the wind was still whipping the snow until it covered all directions and it was impossible to tell if more was falling or whether it was second-hand snow still on the move, inside there was a sense of peace. If we ignored the draughts, some of which were so strong that the carpet rippled.

Something made me climb back up

those steep stairs to the attic. Low windows threw a little light in now the snow had been blown from the ledges and I could see the shapes of the boxes stacked there. I went down onto my knees and pulled that little cream box out and took the glass bauble out. I held it on the palm of my hand, feeling the weightlessness that was somehow also immense, and watched the wild light catch the gold lettering. Baby's first Christmas.

Was there a baby that had been forcibly adopted? A miscarriage? Or simply the idea of a baby, the hopes of a husband and family that never came true? I pulled out my phone and went through the details of Aunt Millie's life that I'd got dad to send me. Born in 1922, lived with an ever-decreasing number of siblings and parents, until the death of her frail mother in 1950. No scandals, no 'sending away to the country', no family whispers of shame or secrecy, just a lady living a reclusive life, tucked away in her old house, with a selection of cats for company, until her own death.

Which meant that whoever the love of her life had been, he must have happened after her mother's death in 1950, otherwise something would have reached the ears of the rest of the family. And the bauble had been bought in pounds, shillings and pence, so it had happened before decimalisation. Well, that narrowed things down a bit, I thought, letting the bauble spin at the end of its narrow ribbon. A ribbon that had never been tied at the top, never formed a loop that could hang on a tree. *Never born* . . .

'Oh, there you are.' Toby pushed a pile of vegetables into my hands when I went back into the kitchen. 'I was thinking you'd fallen into that demon dimension which, temperature notwithstanding, I am still certain is whirling about in that spare bedroom. Here. Peel as if your very life depended upon it. Which, if we've got demons, it very well might.' A potato peeler of uncertain vintage was thrust into my other hand.

One of the lads put their phone on the worktop and began playing music through it. He started with rap, at which we all shuffled uncomfortably, as if the essence of 'slightly sheltered old lady' had seeped into the walls and was protesting, silently, at the use of 'language'. He moved through some country and western, which was too twangy and intrusive, to eventually settle on ABBA, as a comfortable compromise. I peeled potatoes, carefully not commenting on the fact that the villagers had clearly shopped a lot earlier than Toby, because these gave the impression of having been nibbled by mice. I cut the worst bits off and reasoned that we'd be boiling them anyway and that 'Dancing Queen' performed falsetto by three men was probably killing all known germs.

The contrast to last Christmas Eve was particularly marked now. That had been hushed, tasteful plainsong played over speakers as we hosted Simon's friends and neighbours in the carefully decorated flat. No holly branches, no mistletoe, just a few well-placed candles amid the sterile purity. Definitely no linked-arm dancing to 'Voulez Vous', while sorting sprouts, and Toby's rendition of 'Gimme Gimme Gimme', complete with grasping gestures, which would have given Simon seizures.

Eventually Toby declared that all the prep was done. Daylight was beginning to fade from the windows but that didn't diminish the rattle of the panes as the wind carried on its assault. From far below we could hear the waves thumping against the shore and even indoors the air smelled of salt. I went to the front door and pulled it open against the wind, looking down the road at the lit windows in the houses and the way the snow's surface was being scoured clear again. 'It looks like an advent calendar out there.' Toby peered out past my shoulder.

There was another noise now, a kind of whine above the sound of the wind, and a light sweeping up the street. 'What the hell is that?' Kieran had come to stand with us now. 'It's like some strange flying contraption.'

'It is, Mister Eighteen Twenty, it's a bloody helicopter.' Patrick pushed his head into the remaining gap. 'They'll be flying food in, and essential supplies for vulnerable people. And that's parents with small children and the elderly, before you get excited.'

'Should we go up and help?' I was already pulling my coat on and preparing my feet for the unpleasant experience of the inside of wet boots. 'Stuff might need carrying.'

'Plus, it's a Navy helicopter. Men in uniform.' Patrick was dragging his coat down from the pegs behind the front door.

'Navy is not a good colour for a helicopter. How would you see it in the sky?' But Kieran joined the general melee of booting and suiting, and we slithered our, now expert, way down the steps and onto the hill. The sound of the helicopter had brought other people out now, random shapes in burly coats were all making their way up the slope, a whole crowd of us drifting up towards the noise of rotor blades and engine.

The helicopter had put down on a flattish field that might possibly have been the village football pitch in better weather. It stood there, rotors still going and nobody appearing for a few minutes, snow agitated into devils by the blades, while we all formed a sort of jostling mass at a sensible distance for a while. 'Yeah, great, very decorative and everything, but we need fresh milk,' muttered someone. 'I hope it's a genuine mission and not some bloody training exercise.'

Like a scene from *Close Encounters*, the door opened slowly, letting a shaft of light spill out onto the whirling snow, bright against the rapid coming of night, and a couple of figures wearing what looked like flight suits emerged. One began unloading boxes, upon which the villagers fell eagerly, the other

7

After a pause long enough to feel really awkward, he turned his smile on. 'Well, aren't you going to introduce me to your friends?' And there, right there was that tone. That oh-so-reasonable tone that made me feel rude and anti-social and misplaced.

'Oh, yes, sorry. This is Patrick and Kieran. You already know Toby. This is Simon. My ex fiancé.'

It wasn't even worth asking him how he'd hitched a ride on a helicopter. How he'd found me. If Simon wanted something, he would get it, by charm, by stealth . . . my brain was too shocked at the sight of him here to even think the relevant questions . . . by bullying. Patrick shook his hand, Toby just dug his hands further into the pockets of his coat. Kieran had joined the villagers and was manhandling a box of food along the snow towards us.

'Well.' Simon looked satisfied. 'Now I've finally got here, where are we heading? Back to your place?' And he set off down the hill, following some people who'd already shouldered their box of supplies and were heading off into the village. Toby stared at me.

'You told him?' He had hold of my elbow, and was using it to stop me from walking after Simon.

'No! I had no idea . . . I *still* have no idea how he did this!' I was fighting a rising tide of indignation, anger and some nameless emotions that swirled around my head like the wind-blown snow. Toby's assumption that I'd been in touch with Simon, after all I'd said, hurt more than the stinging little particles of ice. 'He must have got it out of my parents.'

'Well.' Toby let go of my arm. 'What now, Matz?'

'I don't know.' I dropped my voice. 'Murder is still illegal, right?'

'Afraid so. Smarmygiticide, they'd

call it, and everyone would understand but, yup, against the law.'

'I don't want him in my house.'

Toby made a face. 'Well, that's a given. What do we do?'

There was a limping, dragging sound and Kieran, box on his shoulder, caught up with us. Patrick was trailing along in the wake of Simon, clearly undecided what to do, given my lukewarm response to his arrival, whilst Simon was blazing his way confidently down the hill towards what I was beginning to realise was my sanctuary. It might be a cold, draughty, cat-smelling badly decorated barn of a place, but it was *mine* and I was buggered if I'd let Simon the Vane start putting his 'damned-with-faint-praise' mark all over it.

'We have to stop him getting in.'

'Got that.' Kieran put the box down and pulled out his mobile. After a second his call was answered by Patrick further down the hill. 'Stop him before he gets to the house.'

We heard the affirmative answer.

'How would he know which house was yours?' Toby asked.

'Knowing Simon he'll have Googlemapped it. He's probably got the floor plans and paint and fabric samples too.' I gritted my teeth. 'It's what he does. He kind of moves in and takes over. If we let him in, he'll have had it redesigned and built himself a garden studio before we get through the front door.'

'He can only do what you let him, though, Matz,' Toby said. He reached out and took my hand, pulling it from my coat pocket, where it was bunched in a fist that wanted to punch Simon so hard that he'd crash land out of Belgian airspace, but wouldn't. Would never dare. 'He's only got as much power over you as you give him.' Toby's fingers were warm as they laced with mine. His palm burned into mine. 'And he's had everything from you that you are ever going to give, right?'

It wasn't the firmness of his tone. It wasn't the feel of my hand in his. It wasn't any of the things I could reason myself out of. It was because it was *Toby*. Because he'd been there and he'd seen the damage Simon had done to me, and he still knew I was Mattie. The Mattie I'd always been, underneath.

'He hasn't had the arse-kicking that I am about to give him, though, has he?'

And Toby turned to me. 'You are so right about that,' he said, and dropped a gentle kiss on my lips. It was the first time he'd ever shown any sign of wanting to kiss me, and it came without the warning I usually expected, so my lips were dry and cold. I hadn't had chance to so much as run my tongue over them. 'Bloody hell,' he said. 'I think you might already be dead.'

And all I could feel was the rush of blood, singing in my ears and making my heart kick in my chest like a bolshy pony.

Kieran's phone beeped. 'The subject is in the vicinity of the house,' he reported.

'Tell Patrick not to let him in.' Toby's kiss was still heavy on my lips. It weighted me down, gave me a sense of gravity and a centre. 'Don't give him any reasons, he'll just turn it all round.'

Instructions were relayed. 'You don't have to face him, you know,' Toby said, very matter-of-factly. 'Go home, lock yourself in. He'll get the message.'

'Only after six weeks or so. Trust me, Simon doesn't get any message that doesn't have an invitation from the Palace wrapped round it. I have to talk to him.'

'He won't see what he's done. He can't. He is who he is, he thinks his behaviour is normal.' Toby sounded quite worried now.

I gave his hand a squeeze. 'I'm not going to show him the error of his ways, Toby. I'm going to get closure for myself.'

We'd reached the house by now. Patrick was standing outside looking bemused, and Simon was leaning against the wall, completely at ease.

'Come on now, Mattie,' he said, all big beaming smile and bonhomie. 'You'd far rather invite me in for a cup of tea than have me stand out here and air your dirty laundry in public, wouldn't you?'

'It's hypnotism,' Toby whispered. 'Don't look into the eyes.'

'No, Simon, you are not coming in,' I said firmly.

He made a lips-pursed-sad face, like a mother whose toddler is wilfully disobeying. 'Tch.' Then an appeal to everyone. 'Look, I think we can all agree that Matilda isn't herself at the moment, I'm thinking it's some sort of breakdown. Nobody in their right mind would run from a beautiful home and a fiancé who loves her more than life itself, would they?' He stepped in closer. 'Come on, Mattie. Come back to London with me. We can get you proper treatment, a nice quiet stay somewhere out of town and you'll be right as rain in no time.'

'No,' I said, and started up the steps

to the front door, with Patrick and Toby on either side of me. Kieran laboured up after us with the box still balanced across his shoulder. We carefully kept to the side of the steps, practice now telling us where to put our feet to avoid sliding back down, and reached the top to look down on Simon, who was still leaning against the wall at the bottom. He had on a 'go on, you know you're only going to give in and let me do as I want anyway' expression on his face, but I ignored it. 'Go home, Simon. It's over.'

A sigh. 'Oh no, my dear. I beg to differ.' He ran a hand through his hair, primping. Simon was always very conscious of how he looked. He knew the flight suit made him look impressively military, and I'd take any bets he'd practised that insouciant walk in it. From a distance I heard the sound of 'Once in Royal David's City'. It was approaching us. The village choir must have turned straight out after the supplies had been unpacked, and

156

decided to start at the top of the hill, with my house.

I could see the light of candles in lanterns, guttering and flicking in the wind. 'That's either carol singers or a mob with blazing torches,' Toby whispered beside me. Simon was on the bottom step now, still smiling. He clearly thought his words were getting through, that my reluctance to go indoors was born of a desire to hear him out, to give in, to run back to him and that life of caged sumptuousness that was really no life at all.

'Come on, Mattie,' he said, and his tone was so level, so *reasonable* that I felt the men beside me on the doorstep shifting about uncomfortably. They were doing what my friends had done, rewritten their versions of me inside their heads to include all the things that Simon was saying about me. That I was unstable, difficult to live with. That I talked about them behind their backs, spreading gossip and innuendo about the people who'd confided in me.

And then Simon fed it back to me. How my so-called 'friends' laughed about me. How they discussed my failings, pretended to be friendly so that they could have more fuel for their pity and patronising. How they kept me around as a specimen of 'what not to do' to make themselves feel better.

He'd made me believe all that. And more. He'd made me believe things about *myself*, things that I knew weren't true but had come to think might be. That I was weak, no good with money. My clothes were no good, I had no eye for colour, no *style*. That I needed him, with his contacts and his flair and his sheer understanding of the world, to be able to function.

'Once in Royal David's City' stopped, and broke off into shufflings and coughs as the singers toiled up the steep slope, and it suddenly dawned on me that I hadn't salted the steps as promised. If I didn't do something soon there was going to be a terrible untidy mass of people bundling about on my doorstep, and

Simon might well get inside in the resulting melee.

I turned around to head into the kitchen for the rock salt, Toby, Kieran and Patrick standing aside to let me through. At which point a lot of things happened at once. Simon seemed to crack, whether it was the cold or my general refusal to acknowledge him, I didn't know, but the mask which had, admittedly, been wearing a bit thin as he stood there realising, presumably, that I wasn't going to let him in, split completely.

'Don't you turn your back on me you bitch!' He screamed the words, and a general air of quiet listening descended from the approaching carol singers, who were looming into view now as a mass of bundled shapes, some wrapped in the multi-coloured wool garments that told me they were customers of Thea's. 'You *will* let me in and you *will* listen to me!'

Simon set off up the steps, and even in the vague light that shone from inside the house, I could see his face was twisted and bent with rage. His mouth was wide, his teeth bared and his hands held out in front of him as though he wanted to tear me apart. Every instinct told me to run into the house, lock the door, shut him out. Reason with him through the letterbox if necessary, tell him I knew how wrong I'd been, apologise, take the silence and the ignoring that would result until he decided I was once more fit to socialise with.

But I didn't. I stood at the top of the steps, my face raised to the sky, and let him come. I had no idea what I was going to do when he arrived, of course, but I knew Simon, and I knew that he would make his loss of the mask my fault, somehow. That cold reason would come back down onto his features and I would be made to feel half a centimetre high.

I hadn't allowed for the sheer iciness of those steps and, clearly, Simon hadn't either. He made it just past half-way, propelled by anger, before his feet must have landed on a particularly glassy patch, because his boots shot from underneath him. He twisted, his expression now more one of surprise that the natural word dared to rise against the might of Simon Vane, and shot back down the stairway on his backside, his hands desperately grasping out to try to catch at the undergrowth, but missing all the bushes. He arrived on the road at the feet of the carol singers, turned and tried to stand, but the ice and snow was too compacted and he was moving too fast to get any purchase. There was a second of scrabbling where it looked as though he might have grabbed at someone's ankle and managed to slow himself, but his momentum was such that he couldn't get up, just flailed a bit, and then was taken by the gradient again, whisked off down the hill towards the harbour at an impressive velocity.

'Shall we wait for the comedy

splash?' Toby said, after a second.

'He . . . ' I gasped, trying to get air in past the shock. 'He'll be injured!'

'He called you a bitch. Bit of injury is definitely called for, I'd say.' Toby gently pushed the front door open. A burst of light spilled out onto the snow. 'Besides, he's wearing a flight suit. He'll be fine.'

'Assuming he doesn't slide right on into the harbour and drown.' It was Kieran's voice that made me realise what had really happened. Kieran and Patrick and Toby, and all those members of the village that Simon didn't know . . . they'd all seen it. Simon's total loss of control and then his loss of dignity and face as he'd careered down the main street towards the sea. It was his worst nightmare — being shown up in front of people he didn't know. People he hadn't had a chance to impress yet with his 'better than you' education and financial situation, people who didn't know that he owned a flat in a prestigious London location, that he'd gone to Eton . . . and now, people who didn't care. People who would always think of him as 'that prat that fell down the steps'. And, because he didn't know them, he couldn't even begin to influence them, couldn't tell them that 'that bitch deliberately made the steps icy', because they wouldn't believe him.

Simon had looked a complete idiot, and that would utterly infuriate him, but he was completely unable to do anything about it.

Down on the road the carol singers broke into a slightly ragged version of 'Oh Little Town of Bethlehem', clearly deciding not to attempt the steps, but then, we were all standing outside anyway, so there was no point. We then got two verses of 'The First Noel', after which I scuttered down to the street and put a fiver in their tin. They shuffled off and we could hear their footsteps cracking and scuffing through the snow as they headed back to civilisation, the lights of their candles and lanterns dim amid the wind-blown drifts.

In the light I could see a faint outline, climbing the hill but keeping to the shadows, hiding in a gateway to avoid being illuminated as the carol singers shuffled past it through the snow. *Simon*. It had to be. I glanced once more, briefly, over my shoulder as I went carefully back up the steps, the figure was labouring slowly upwards back towards the helicopter landing field. I hoped they'd waited for him, it would be a long limp back to London for him otherwise.

8

'Well, that was fun.' We all clambered into the hallway to be met by a gust of warm air. The range was clearly still doing its job. There was even a faint smell of cooking drowning out the overwhelming 'cat'. 'If he turns up again we just point and laugh and ask if he's thought about joining the three-man bobsleigh team.' Toby put out an arm to gather me in to the little study. 'Do you think it's over, Matz?'

I thought for a moment. 'Yes. I don't think he'll bother with me now. I've seen him at his most vulnerable and he won't want to be reminded of that.' I flexed my shoulders. A weight seemed to have gone, my heart felt lighter as though someone had tied balloons to it. 'And I've realised that he was a complete plonker. I mean, he always was, but he could talk his way out of it by making me feel insecure. I doubt very much if even *Simon* could put a spin on sliding out of the village on his bum. And the best thing is that he did it to himself. If he hadn't come charging up those steps intent on telling everyone what a bitch I was . . . well.' I held out my hands.

'Please tell me that, if he hadn't, you still wouldn't have got back with him.' There was a little worried crease between Toby's eyes. 'You wouldn't have been that mad.'

I laughed. 'Nope. That bubble is well and truly burst.'

There was a knock on the front door and we froze like cartoon characters. 'D'you think that's him?' Toby rubbed his face. 'Shall I go out there and punch him?'

'He wouldn't.' I went towards the door. 'But, in the event he *would*, I am prepared to shove him back down those steps again.'

'That's my girl,' Toby said, very quietly. I wasn't sure he meant me to hear, it was that kind of undertone that sounded as though it was how he talked to himself, so I pretended I hadn't. But anyway, it wasn't Simon on the doorstep, it was Thea, wearing what looked like a knitted boiler suit. Big blocks of primary colours covered both her legs, and both arms were green. 'Blimey, you look like a bar chart,' Toby said, and I realised he'd never properly met Thea and her wool-orientated sense of fashion.

'Those steps are killer,' she said, slightly out of breath. 'Oh, and that bloke that came down arse first, anything to do with you?'

'My ex,' I said, and stood back to let her into the hallway.

'Uh huh. Jerk.' I wasn't sure if that was a comment or an instruction, so I stood quietly hoping it would become apparent. 'Total tosspot.' Since we were clearly on the same wavelength, I ushered her inside and we all went into the kitchen, where it was warm and smelled of something cooking. Thea looked around. 'Wow. It's like a time-warp,' she said. 'You staying here?'

'I'd like to. Might turn it into a B&B.'

She nodded slowly. 'Good call.' I made a face at Toby when she wasn't looking. Kieran, either smitten or blinded by the outfit, pulled a stool out for Thea alongside where he and Patrick were sitting at the work surface. 'Need some new people in Steepleton, it's, like, everyone's lived here since forever and they've all run out of things to talk about.'

'Maybe you could help me with the interior design?' The idea surprised me, but not as much as it clearly surprised Thea. 'You know, some of your cushion covers in those lovely sea colours would be just right when we get the place done up. And maybe some throws and things?'

Thea looked delighted. 'That would show those old biddies who thought I was wasting my time going off to college! Is it going to be all, like, boutique then? Could do with something a bit classy round here, it's mostly chintz and china.' She sighed. 'And I should know, my mum runs one. It'll really naff her up if I go to work with a rival.' A pause, while she looked around and took in the sheer volume of men in the kitchen. 'It's more like the Chippendales in here.'

All three men straightened their shoulders and stuck out their chests a bit, clearly flattered to be compared to a bunch of male strippers, though I didn't know why. Simon had once told me I looked like a stripper, when I'd worn a shortish skirt, and it had been anything but a compliment. 'Well, early days yet.'

Thea was looking as though she'd fallen into some form of heaven. But I suppose, being surrounded by a bunch of men that she hadn't known since playgroup probably came pretty close — even though one of them was gay, one was engaged and the other was . . . well . . . he was *Toby*.

'I've spoken to my gran,' Thea said, when she'd stopped gazing around her.

'She rang just before we came carol singing, and I asked her about your aunt, y'know, if she'd had a bloke or anything.'

I felt myself straighten and my spine prickle. 'What did she say?'

She pushed her hands up inside that primary coloured romper suit. It looked like something Toby would wear on a work night. 'She didn't really know much,' she said, with a shrug. 'Sorry. She just said that your aunt sometimes used to go a bit 'misty' she called it, and go on about 'secrets in the attic' and all that shit.'

Disappointment bit hard. The bauble. 'Yes, we found that one. Oh well, never mind, thanks for trying.'

Thea got up. 'Yeah, okay, no worries. Better go and catch up with the 'Come All Ye Faithful' brigade, they'll be thinking I fell into the harbour. We've got the rest of the village to do yet.' And she was gone, out into the night of whirling wind and second-hand snow being blown around in little tornadoes,

170

like ghosts forming and reforming. As I opened the front door to let her out the gust of air that her leaving let in was icy, bit around noses and fingers until it dissipated in the warmth of the house.

'Well, that's a shame.' Toby was beside me again, in the hallway now. He looked more streamlined now he'd lost the big jumper, and the pricks of stubble had grown into something approaching a dusting of beard that made his cheekbones look strong and rugged. I looked at him. 'What? Matz? What's the matter?'

It was as if the Toby I'd known for all these years; the Toby who'd been my best friend, my confidante, my colourfully-dressed sidekick, had gone. Instead, here was a stranger. One with broader shoulders, longer fingers, greener eyes . . . 'Sorry. Nothing. So, Aunt Millie went on about secrets in the attic. We've already found the bauble, so . . . dead end, I guess.'

'And you're okay?' He was so close now that his words tickled my skin. 'You're sure? When you got up to open that door, I wasn't sure what you were going to do. What if it had been Simon? You didn't feel sorry for him, want to go and kiss him better? Not even for a second?'

Toby. Toby who had always been there. 'Why didn't you ever try to stop me? Some of those idiots I went out with, why did you never say anything?'

He looked a bit embarrassed. Gave his head a sort of half-jerk as though he wanted to turn away but didn't dare, and looked quickly behind us into the kitchen, where Patrick and Kieran were fiddling with the little tree. 'Because you were my friend. And I'd rather have you as a friend, have you around in my life, than have you storming out and never speaking to me again because I told you you were going out with the cross between David Brent from *The Office* and . . . and . . . ' He closed his eyes as he seemed to be mentally searching for a suitably obnoxious simile . . . 'and . . . some leering sex pest, the name of whom escapes me.'

The venom of his words took me aback. 'Some of them were okay,' I said, feebly.

'They weren't *me* though, were they?' he said, with a rueful little smile. 'And I wanted it to be me, Matz.'

'You should have . . . '

'I refer you to my previous answer.' He put his hands on my shoulders. 'I would rather have you in my life as a friend, than not at all.'

In the background, Kieran cleared his throat. 'I, um, I hate to interrupt, but . . . ' We snapped apart. 'Do you think we should stand the tree up on the table? Then we can put presents underneath it without risking spinal torsion.' He waved a hand, indicating the lower branches of the tiny tree, which were practically on the floor.

'We'll look like we're having a hobbit Christmas,' I said. 'But, yeah, go for it. I'm going to have a hot bath and go to bed.' I wanted to lie still in a dark room and possibly replay that image of Simon slithering down the main street in front of the entire village. I felt mean about it, but it was still, possibly, one of the best moments in my life. Karma didn't usually deliver when anyone was watching.

9

I lay in my sleeping bag listening to Toby breathing softly. Toby, who'd kissed me. Toby who wanted to be more than friends. Who'd been there for me. Who I was gradually starting to see as a man.

I'd been so blind. So stupidly assuming, as though I'd only ever taken in the superficial details. Not seen Simon for what he really was, or Toby either for that matter, just slid over their surfaces, of what they purported to be; a rich, intense, stylish but loving partner and . . . a best friend who only wanted me to be happy.

The springs in the narrow mattress plinged under my back as I shifted, letting in a few gusts of air, cool now we'd let the range die down, to chill the heat of embarrassment and shame. If you compared the two men, in fact, if you compared Toby to *any* of my previous partners, it was always a case of the steadfast and constantly good-humoured against the mercurial, the highly-strung and artistic. Good friend as opposed to the good to be seen with. I blushed so hard that, had he been awake, Toby could have read a book by the light of my face.

Why hadn't I seen it? And was it too late now, to do anything about it?

I glanced over at the other bed. By the faint light which filtered in through the wind-blown snow which hung, like dusty net curtains across the window, I could see Toby's profile. A face I had known for years. Trusted for years. Who was — although I was only coming to realise it slowly — bloody good-looking, with a body that was so sexy it was surprising he hadn't already melted the mainland clear. But never mind him, I trusted him implicitly — could I trust myself not to make another stupid mistake?

Oh this was getting us nowhere. I got

up, the cold nibbling into me like hungry mice, and pulled on some clothes. I inched my way out of the room and along the whinging floor-boards of the landing, where I stood for a moment. From somewhere came the sound of a church ringing in Christmas Day, the bell clear through the quiet night air, and I made my decision to go upwards rather than down. To take that little glass bauble and hang it on our tiny tree in memory of my great-aunt, in memory of whatever loss she had endured. Blocking out the sound of ribald snores from the archaeologists, I made my way along the chilly corridor and up that bare set of stairs to the attic.

The bleak little dormer window let in enough light for me to see the three boxes on the floor, and I bent down with my back against the plaster of the wall. 'Sorry, Aunt Millie,' I whispered into the air. 'I can't find those 'boys'. I've got nothing to go on . . . and I feel stupid and naïve and like I can't even trust myself to choose a decent man.'

'Don't be so hard on yourself.' The answer came in a high-pitched squeak, which made me jump really hard and nearly drop the box of decorations that I'd hauled onto my lap. 'I think you know you're onto a winner with that Toby, don't you?' He'd followed me.

'You absolute bugger.'

'Sorry. I woke up and saw you leaving the room. Was a bit worried that you might . . . well, I knew you'd be beating yourself up over Simon-the-Twonk and his incredible Slalom action, so I thought I'd come and talk you down.' He came further into the attic. 'Wow. I've never seen an attic so tidy. Where are all the boxes of Victorian china and old budgie-cages?' Another slow spin. 'And, more to the point, where is the mad old woman? Apart from you, I mean, obviously.' His hands flickered. 'I want *atmosphere*! I want fluttering rags, I want half-heard laughter!' He opened one of the boxes and rummaged, pulling out the old coat I'd previously seen, some ancient dresses in horrible floral fabric and a large knitted jumper, then sneezed several times in succession. 'I want antihistamines!'

'I think Aunt Millie just wasn't sentimental about stuff,' I said.

'Then *why* . . . ?' Toby held up the jumper. It was huge, knitted in several colours but all of them far more muted and subtle than Thea's. It looked *genuine* somehow, ' . . . did she hang on to *this*?'

I found myself running a finger over the knitted surface. It had gone all bobbly with age and wear, the wool under the arms had been re-stitched in a different colour and one of the cuffs was coming slowly unravelled. 'She probably wore it. It looks pretty warm.'

He looked at me with his head sideways. 'You're thinking of the place when we first came the other day. It wouldn't have been *that* cold when your aunt was here, that range belts out the heat like a fiery hell furnace, complete with little pokey devils.'

'Maybe she only wore it outside then.'

'So why is it up here in a box and not on the hook behind the door? That's where her coat and hat are.' He sneezed again. 'Plus, it's bloody enormous. Unless your aunt could give Robbie Coltrane a run for his money, it must have hung to her ankles and, while I'm sure Christmas Steepleton isn't exactly Paris in the fashion stakes, she couldn't have worn this outside even if she wanted. You'd never get down those steps in something like this. You'd have to walk like someone had stapled your knees together.' He stopped rooting around and came over to where I sat crouched over the decorations box, then slid down so he sat next to me on the boards. 'Mattie.'

'Yes?'

'Would you do me the honour of agreeing to go out with me? Just as a kind of trial run thing, you know, see if we're compatible. Maybe dinner, a few

drinks, take it from there sort of thing?'
He was looking at the floor, not at me.
His hair was brushed forward by sleep,
all flat and straggly, and he had never
looked handsomer.

'I think that sounds most charming,
Mister Wilson.' I leaned closer and
nudged him. 'I'm sorry, Toby. I don't
know why I didn't see it before.'

A casual arm came around my
shoulders. 'You weren't seeing me. You
were seeing Professor Pat-a-Cake and
his amazing balloon circus. Incidentally,
I trained up making inflated condom
animals whilst we were at uni, so, you
know, that degree wasn't *totally* wasted.'

'Plus, I'm an idiot who can't see
what's in front . . . oh.'

'Matz?' Out of the corner of my eye I
saw him turn his head to look properly
at me now. 'Are you okay?'

Using the wall and Toby's shoulder to
lever myself to my feet, I got up and
went over to the other box. It was half
covered with discarded clothing that
he'd thrown from the 'Cloths' box, and

I carefully pulled it free. 'I've just been saying words, Toby. Not seeing what's going on, not properly.'

'Matz, you're scaring me now. Is our dating still on?' He stood up too.

'Oh yes.' I took a couple of steps towards him. 'Most definitely.'

'Well. That's all right then. I find myself slightly reassured. I was going to have a shave and everything, and I'd hate to waste the effort.' He ran a finger over his cheek. 'And the resultant sink cleaner.'

Now I took another small step in and kissed him. A proper, firm kiss, my hands against his chest, feeling his heart go from steady, regular pulsing to hammering. He smelled of the shower-gel/dust/warm smell of sleep but he tasted ripe and exciting, which was weird. I'd never associated Toby with excitement before, almost as if he had no corners I couldn't see around. But now, here he was, hinting of unknown things, of potentials and other things which sent a little tremor down my back, and this was a kiss unlike any other kiss ever.

When I stepped back, we were both breathing hard and slightly wider eyed than we had been.

'Well,' I said, and my voice had gone down a couple of octaves. 'Well.' I cleared my throat.

'That's a very deep well,' he said. 'I mean . . . no, I don't. Anyway. You were previously getting all hinty about something I am clearly missing?'

'Oh.' That kiss had distracted me completely, and made my brain feel as though it was leaning sideways. 'Yes! Yes I did.' And I crossed the floor to the other box, the one labelled 'Payprs'. 'Look at this place, Toby.'

Toby looked around. 'Okay, yes, boards, dust, windows, boxes. Got it.'

'Aunt Millie didn't keep stuff. She just didn't. The bedrooms are pretty bleak, and she didn't seem to hoard anything.'

'Apart from cobwebs. She must have had a pretty hardcore attitude to those.'

He ran his hands through his hair. 'And cat ornaments.'

'So then . . . why . . . ' I upended the box and the smell of old newsprint spilled out, accompanied by a pile of paper, ' . . . would she keep a box of newspapers?'

Toby screwed up his face. 'For cleaning? Well, all right, admittedly there's not a lot of brass to polish, but maybe . . . maybe she shoved it in the windows?'

'Then why have the box in the attic?' I began sifting through the papers. They were complete editions, not clippings, and all of them were old. 'And why would they all be from the same week? It's like she kept all the editions of all the papers for . . . ' I flicked the first couple open, ' . . . the beginning of February 1953.'

Toby joined me and we spread out all the newspapers. There were about twenty, mostly local papers but also some national ones, and all the front pages seemed concerned with the same thing. VIOLENT STORMS CLAIM HUNDREDS OF LIVES. Toby got his phone out and hit Google, while I skim read the first pages of all the papers.

'1953. North Sea surge, high tide, massive storms.' Toby mumbled, reading from his screen. 'London flooded, Eastern sea defences washed out . . . etc etc.'

My skin was pricking all over. I could feel the hairs on the back of my neck rising. The most represented newspaper there seemed to be *The Steepleton, Peytonbury and Woodchurch Advertiser*, which had a morning and afternoon edition, as I found when I stacked the papers into a more orderly form. The front page, during that week, told a story of wild, high tides, sea defences breached, fields flooded, livestock drowned. And a boat, a small fishing boat, the 'Mary-Anne', out of Christmas Steepleton . . .

I raked through the copies, once I'd got my eye in I found I could pick the name out of columns of newsprint.

'Listen. The Mary-Anne had been out fishing, the storm came up, she tried to get back to harbour and sank, with the loss of all on board.'

Toby scrabbled some more copies. 'The boat gets a mention in this one too. And . . . here, this paper . . . oh, and the *Daily Mirror* here — 'one of the ships lost was the Mary-Anne from Christmas Steepleford' — wow, misprints are nothing new then, 'which sank with all hands on board, only yards from the safety of the harbour.'' He looked at me, eyes shadowed. 'She kept all the papers that mentioned that night, that boat sinking.'

I scrabbled again, flicking through until I found the final copy of the *Advertiser*. Dated the fifth of February, it was the only one from that day. The storm had pretty much passed from the local headlines by then, although Google told us that London was still clearing up and burying the dead, most headlines were reporting the end of sweet rationing. Only the *Advertiser* that she'd kept was covering the continuing search for the bodies of the four men who'd been crewing the Mary-Anne.

'Google says 'The Mary-Anne, from Christmas Steepleton, was lost in the storm of 1953 on the night of 31 January. On board were Henry Gass, Albert Dike, Jim Pettinger and Walter Cross. All hands lost, and their bodies never recovered.' That's all, but the Princess Victoria sank in the same storm and that was the biggest loss of life since the war, so everyone covered that rather than the loss of fishing boats.'

'That's a fisherman's sweater.' I found I was whispering. 'In with the clothes. One of those men ... ' I stopped. I could feel the words but they wouldn't come out of my mouth.

'They were trying to get back to the harbour.' Toby, staring at his phone screen, sounded as shocked as though it had just happened. 'Running for the safety of Christmas Steepleton. And they nearly made it.'

A blast of wind shook the windows and we both jumped. The impact of the fact that everything had been right in front of me and I hadn't seen it, was sinking in slowly. Not just Toby, but these boxes. I had never bothered to look inside properly. I'd scanned the surface, found it okay but not exciting, and that had been as far as I went. 'Toby, I'm sorry.' Tears bulged in my throat. 'I should have seen.'

'Hey, hey. I hide my light under a bushel, whatever that is but when I find one I'll know because it will have my light under it.' He stepped in and wrapped his arms around me. 'And these?' I heard a toe scrape one of the piles of papers. 'How could you have known? It's a bloody attic not a pinboard.' A hug that tightened and I could feel his cheek against the top of my head. 'I'm just glad you've seen it now.' A sigh. 'And by 'it', I mean me, although obviously I am glad that you've also found out something about your great-aunt.'

'Boys.' I said suddenly. 'In memory of her lost love. Boys, Toby.'

'Well, it's more girls for me, but a lot of people make that mistake, it must be the way I walk or something.'

I stepped out of his hug and looked up into his face. 'Boys. But it's not, is it? It's not B.O.Y.S, it's B.U.O.Y.S. She wanted her ashes scattered over the markers of the safe harbour, in memory of the sailors, or one of them, I don't know if we'll ever find out which one it was.'

'She didn't know it was spelled differently.' Toby's voice was a bit hushed now. 'She wrote it the way it sounded. And I don't suppose it matters which one it was, does it. Really? They sailed together and died together, and they might all have left someone behind, mourning them. So we can scatter those ashes in memory of all of them.'

'And in memory of lives that never would be.' I bent down and took the glass bauble from its box. 'Whether she was pregnant or just hoping to be ... Aunt Millie would have been thirty-one when that boat sank. She never married, never had children, but she was a bloody good aunt to my dad, I know that. She was old when I knew her, but she was always pleased to see me. She stayed single. So she really must have been devastated when he died.' I imagined it, a night like this, the whole village out on the clifftops, willing the Mary-Anne to make it to safe harbour; the collective silence and grief when she foundered just beyond the reach of that curved sea wall. Great-aunt Millie, not the bowed and dubiously-polyestered lady I'd known distantly, a supplier of lollies who'd let me stroke her cats and cuddle kittens when we visited, but a strong, upright thirty-year-old woman, with hopes and a future all planned. Maybe she'd be saving for her wedding, maybe she was hoping breathlessly for a proposal, maybe it had all gone further than that and it would be a quick wedding and a 'honeymoon baby' . . .

'We can scatter the ashes in the morning,' Toby said. 'If the wind has dropped, obviously, otherwise there's not much point, she'll get back to the house faster than we will.' The wind thumped around us again, storming down the street like an out of control elephant. 'But for now, bed.'

'First I'm going to put this bauble on the tree though,' I said, holding it up on the palm of my hand. 'Now we've got it figured out, sort of. I don't think it's something to be hidden, we should hang it and remember her.'

'Good idea. We can bring it out every year and put it out in memory of . . . oh, and I realise I have jumped several guns there. But, you know, hoping there's going to be a lot of Christmases in our future. Together, I mean, not random Christmases. And, here and now, I promise that next Christmas will be better planned and with a bigger tree.'

'In this house?' I hesitated on my way to the stairs.

'Why not? If you want to. I can Professor Pat-a-Cake from here, like you said, lots of Londoners weekending in those cottages, some of them might want children's parties, plus, well, the competition is probably a bit less tough out here. Got to say, Matz, I was getting tired of keeping up with the balloon giraffe Joneses back in town. I was never going to be able to master the triple dachshund with the double poodle loop.' A deep breath. 'And, of course, the qualifier, if our dates go sufficiently well for you to want to set up home with a failed actor who just suspects that he might make an excellent front-of-house man for your B&B business. Separate rooms, if necessary.'

'You,' I said, my voice sounded fierce, even to me, 'are not a failed anything, Toby.'

'Well, I am presently failing to get you to go back to bed, so . . . ' He did a comedy shrug, holding his hands up. 'So let's go and hang this bauble and then get another few hours' sleep.'

The kitchen was very quiet. We didn't turn on the light, just quietly hung the bauble by the blue-ish illumination of the moonlight on the snow outside. There was something very 'otherworld' about it, even the tree had joined in the supernatural vibe and looked twinkly, the milk bottle decorations twisting and turning and catching the reflections.

'Technically, since it's Christmas Day, I can give you your present,' I said, as we stood back to admire the way the bauble pulled the whole of one side of the tree down, as if it'd had some kind of timber-based stroke.

'You've got me a present?' Toby tilted his head. I wasn't sure if that was because he didn't believe me or whether he was trying to straighten up the tree in his eyeline.

'Of course! I always get you a Christmas present!'

'Well, yes, but last year . . . ' He tailed

off. Last year I'd bought him an expensive bottle of some smelly stuff he liked, but Simon had found it and refused to let me hand it over. Simon had worn it himself and I'd had to buy Toby a bottle of supermarket champagne and drop it at his flat while he wasn't in. Simon had come with me, to check. At that point I'd still thought it was a mark of how much he cared about me.

'That was last year. This year, it's different.' We looked at each other across that magically lit kitchen, whilst the range made portentous ticking sounds, either cooling down or about to explode.

'Yes. It is.'

Moments of silence stretched until Toby broke them. 'Okay, presents now. Let's do it.'

'And when you say 'let's do it', you mean . . . ?'

He blushed and the blue light made his face a curious purple shade. 'Oh. Ah, I wasn't suggesting . . . come on,

Matz, you know me! If ever there was a man who wouldn't suggest sex as a Christmas present, then I am he, and I want you to notice the correct grammatical construction of that sentence as a way of distracting you from how embarrassed I am right now.'

I gave his shoulder a gentle punch. 'Have you lost the ability to tell when I'm teasing you?'

A sudden, rather stern look, which didn't sit easily on those friendly, open features, or under that tousled blond hair. 'I've just forgotten what it's like to have a Mattie who teases. I thought I'd lost you.' And there he was, hugging me so hard that I could hear my ribs squeaking and my breath clattered out in a whoosh. 'I thought I'd lost you,' he said, into my hair. 'And this is all I ever wanted to do. To hold you and tell you that everything would be all right even if, on current evidence, that meant squashing you to death.' He slowly released me and took a half step back. 'Is that all right?'

'It's Christmas Day, Toby. Telling me something like that . . . well, I've got the feeling that it means even more because of that.' I very gently stroked the side of his face. 'Now. Presents.'

My jacket was hanging on the back of the door. Now the lads had got the range working I no longer needed to wear it indoors as a kind of front-line defence. I reached into the pocket and drew out the little soft parcel. 'This is yours.'

Toby unwrapped the knitted octopus and greeted it with a joy that seemed slightly out of proportion, but then, so did the octopus. 'Wow! My very own knitted Lovecraftian monster! How ever did you guess?'

'Technically he's a cephalopod not an Old One, but . . . that's pretty much what I was going for. I've been calling him Cthulhu, but you can change his name, I won't mind and he doesn't answer to it or anything.'

'Right.' And he plaited the tentacles for a moment. 'Right. Come with me and I'll show you your present.'

'The werewolf?'

He led me to the unused front room and opened the door. 'Ta da.'

Sitting on a cushion on top of a chair swathed in a dustsheet, was a small grey cat. It looked up when we came in and mewed, then tucked its head in and curled up. I stared at it. 'You were done,' I said. 'Werewolves are bigger.'

Toby began talking very fast. 'After you said about always wanting a pet and you'd get a cat when you moved in, and then they had a board up in the shop and this was the last one of the litter to go — mainly, I suspect, because it's a psychopath — they'll take it back if you don't want it and they're happy to come up and feed it if you need them to and you go back to London but . . . '

I ignored him and went to stroke the cat. It ignored me, but twitched an ear in acknowledgement. 'You're a cutie, aren't you?'

'Don't expect an answer, I've been trying to get him to say happy

Christmas and all I get is purring.' Toby sounded a bit anxious. 'Is it . . . I mean, I wanted to get you something you could keep, a reminder of this . . . ' An arm waved.

Last Christmas. Those bloody diamonds. I'd never wanted diamonds, never asked for them, they were something Simon thought his girlfriend ought to wear. To be suitably decorated, to show off how wealthy, how expansive he was. This . . .

'I've always wanted a cat,' I said slowly. 'Mum's allergic so I could never have one growing up. I always told myself 'when I get my own place, I'll have a cat'. I just . . . ' I cleared my throat. Toby knew this. Of course he did. He listened. 'Thank you. Really. He's adorable.' I considered the curled up ball of silver-grey fluff. 'I'll get to know him better in the morning. I think he's basically telling us it's the middle of the night and to bugger off and get some sleep.'

'And it's really all right?' He still

sounded worried. 'I mean, I know you shouldn't give animals as presents, honestly, but I was at a complete loss and then I saw him . . . ' He tailed off.

'The present isn't the kitten, Toby,' I said quietly. 'It's you showing that you remembered.'

A moment of quiet. 'I remember everything you ever told me, Mattie,' he said. 'Because it mattered. It mattered enough to you to tell me, so it mattered to me.' Then he coughed and swept a hand through his hair. 'Right. Bed, young lady, we've got a busy day tomorrow.'

10

Christmas morning saw a thaw setting in which made the roofs drip and the streets cascade with water as though it was raining from a clear sky. Ice sheets detached and slithered down the hill, with a sound like skiers rushing past and occasional clumps of snow fell from bushes and trees, disturbing the peace and the gulls, which wheeled and hung overhead. The sea had calmed and now just bumped up and down breathily.

We left Patrick and Kieran at the house, arguing over the cooking. I'd given them the two felted figures, who had instantly taken part in a miniature battle, and then set about a table football match using sprouts as a ball when we quietly pulled the door shut behind us. Toby and I tiptoed down the waterfall of the steps and made our way out onto the harbour wall, negotiating the remaining patches of ice carefully, and carrying Aunt Millie's box.

The village was quiet, apart from a family group. Two small children earnestly pedalled new bicycles through the rapidly melting slush along near the shops while their parents leaned indulgently on the railings and watched. Everyone else would still be inside, enjoying Christmas breakfast or in the little church for the carol service, from where the faint sound of an organ played with more gusto than ability drifted.

'Next year, Buck's Fizz and fresh coffee,' Toby muttered, high-stepping through piles of snow. 'If you don't have children, Christmas morning shouldn't start until there are double digits in the day.' A breeze, much warmer than the one we'd got used to, tickled around my ungloved hands. It smelled of new things, of promises and beginnings and also, slightly, of fish.

I crouched down carefully and lifted

the lid of the box. 'Am I doing the right thing? Toby?' I hesitated, the box at an acute angle over the sea, which respired gently beneath us, sucking and blowing at the sea wall in a gentle swell.

'You know you are.' And he bent beside me. 'It feels right. Does it feel right? It feels right to me but then it's not mine, so maybe it would feel like that anyway . . .'

'Yes. Yes it does.' I turned and kissed his cheek, which tasted of salt from the faint spray that was rising with each slap of waves. 'All round, I am doing the right thing.' And I upended the box, letting the wind take Aunt Millie scuttering and dancing, over the row of buoys which ran out from the harbour wall and marked the edge of the safe water before it broke out into the open sea.

'Henry Gass, Albert Dike, Jim Pettinger, Walter Cross.' Toby read the names from his phone as the ashes whirled and curled once more and then faded, either taken by the wind or the sea.

'In memory of all of you,' I said, and straightened up. Toby caught my hand and held it and together we watched as the sun's first rays lifted gently over the clifftops, making the waves glow a rose pink for a moment. There were tears in my eyes, for the lads who never made it home, for Aunt Millie and her disappointed future and a few slightly selfish ones for myself. For the mistakes I'd made and the things I hadn't allowed myself to see.

And then Toby turned to me and kissed me and I felt the weight of my new future, deeper than the sea which splashed approvingly up over our feet, and brighter than this early light of the new day.

'Happy Christmas,' he whispered, and then turned me so we could see the whole village, clinging to the cliffside, embroidered with lights, rooftops just touched with gold. 'Happy new life, Mattie.'

The wind tugged my hair and touched my cheek, and I let myself

Thank you

Thank you so much for reading *The Boys of Christmas*! I hope it's made you feel suitably Christmassy and desirous of sprouts (I really like sprouts, if you haven't yet discovered the joy then try them shredded and fried with bacon, food of the gods I tell you). The village of Christmas Steepleton, sadly, doesn't really exist, although it is loosely based on Lyme Regis in Dorset, where I thoroughly recommend that you visit, although maybe wait until summer . . .

I live in a house not unlike great-aunt Millicent's, big, rambling and mostly unheated, so the bit about trying to sleep wearing a onesie, a fleece and three pairs of socks was based on extensive research conducted during the months of November through until

April. Although I can also vouch for the heating power of two terriers . . .

Can I take this opportunity to wish you a very merry Christmas and a happy New Year? (If you're reading this in June, it still applies, you just have to remember I said it).